"Why have you come back?" Struan demanded

"I want to know the real reason you came here," he went on, "to a dead-end village in the back of nowhere, instead of London where you obviously belong."

"Perhaps I don't want that kind of life anymore," Verity said evenly. "Besides, I've always liked the country." But as she spoke, her eyes on the man she once loved—still loved—Verity knew she was lying.

Had Struan guessed her real purpose? Did he know she still harbored passion for him and that she hoped he too still had feelings for her?

His next words dashed her hopes.

"Let me ask you again, Verity," he said coldly. "Just why are you here? What in heaven's name did you think I might have to offer you now?"

NICOLA WEST, born on the south coast of England, now lives in Central England with her husband and family. She always knew she wanted to write. She started writing articles on many subjects, a regular column in a county magazine, children's stories and women's magazine stories before tackling her first book. Though she had three novels published before she became a Harlequin author, she feels her first novel for Harlequin was a turning point in her career. Her settings are usually places that she has seen for herself.

Books by Nicola West

Don't miss any of our special offers. Write to us at the following address for information on our newest releases.

Harlequin Reader Service
901 Fuhrmann Blvd., P.O. Box 1397, Buffalo, NY 14240
Canadian address: P.O. Box 603,
Fort Erie, Ont. L2A 5X3.

NICOLA WEST

unfinished business

Harlequin Books

TORONTO • NEW YORK • LONDON
AMSTERDAM • PARIS • SYDNEY • HAMBURG
STOCKHOLM • ATHENS • TOKYO • MILAN

Harlequin Presents first edition July 1987
ISBN 0-373-10998-9

Original hardcover edition published in 1986
by Mills & Boon Limited

CHAPTER ONE

'THERE'S a name for women like you,' Hugh said savagely. He stood in the middle of Verity Sandison's spacious, cream-coloured living-room high above London and stared at her, his nostrils flaring a little and white round the edges. 'And it's not a very nice name. Do you know what it is?'

Verity shook her head. For the first time in her life she felt afraid—afraid of Hugh's maleness, of the anger that had been born out of his injured virility. We should have stayed in the restaurant, she thought ruefully, or down in the foyer of the block of flats, anywhere where there were people. Here, alone with a man who had always seemed placid and familiar, and finding him capable of a smouldering and possibly explosive rage, she felt frighteningly vulnerable.

'You don't know?' Hugh persisted, coming a step closer. Verity took a similar step back. Touching her might, in Hugh's present state of mind, be the equivalent of putting a match to touchpaper. 'You surprise me,' he went on with bitter sarcasm. 'I'm amazed nobody's called you by it before. Your previous suitors must have been very tolerant indeed—much more tolerant than I am.' His light brown eyes had darkened, rather as they had darkened only an hour or two ago when he had held her hand over the restaurant table—only then the emotion that had widened his pupils had been a very different one. 'You're a tease, Verity—that's what you are. And the worst kind of tease, too. Because you don't just promise a man the delights of your bed and body for a few hours, or even a few months. No, you're too clever for that. Not only do you hold back yourself, but you make your virginity seem so precious that you make a man ready to hold back too. You make him want to marry you—not just to take you for a mistress, but to share his life with you. To commit himself to you. And only then—when you're got him on his knees, when you've got the ring there in front of you—only then do you draw back and say no. Why, Verity, why?'

Hugh's voice had gradually risen during his impassioned speech, and now he was practically shouting at her, his face only inches away as Verity, unable to back away any further, pressed herself against the wall. 'Don't you understand what it does to a man?' he demanded, gripping her suddenly by the shoulders, his fingers biting cruelly into her tender flesh. 'Don't you have any idea what you're doing?' He stared at her for a few moments, then dropped his hands and turned away with an expression of disgust. 'Well, maybe you do at that. Maybe that's where you get your fun—from watching a man abase himself, watching him squirm when you say no. Maybe when I've gone you'll have another good laugh before going on to the next poor fool to fall for your undeniable beauty.'

Verity stepped away, rubbing her shoulders with trembling hands. Her mouth was dry with fear, but for the moment it seemed that Hugh's normal veneer of urbanity had taken over again, controlling the primitive anger that had shaken him as much as it had shaken her. She shook her head, feeling the tears come to blind her eyes. It wasn't like that at all—but how could she tell him? How could she expect him to believe her?

It was much later when Verity finally stepped under the shower in an effort to wash away the mortification of the evening. The argument had gone on and on, drearily tracking over the same path, treadmilling round the same futile circle until she'd thought she would scream. Not that she'd had to say much—Hugh had done the talking, asking her over and over again why she had done it, why she'd refused his proposal when they'd been getting along so well, when all the pointers had been indicating her acceptance. Why— why—why—if he asked that question once more, she'd thought, she would go mad, completely and irrevocably. Couldn't he *see* that she simply couldn't answer it—at least, in a way that he understood? It seemed that he couldn't, and he was still unsatisfied when he finally shrugged his shoulders and left.

Verity had watched him go with mixed feelings. She'd been fond of Hugh—and yes, she *had* thought she might marry him. She'd certainly never intended to hurt him. But how, she wondered, do you explain your actions to someone else when you don't even understand them yourself?

The water flowed down over her slender back, and Verity tilted her head back to let it soak her hair, turning it from a burnished red-gold to a deep auburn. She lifted its weight away from her naked shoulders, twisting her body and stretching luxuriously under the tingling spray. Thank goodness Hugh's momentary flash of violence hadn't come to anything. She'd been all too aware of her own frailty, matched against his strength; a simple matter of size, her five feet two of slenderness against Hugh's six feet of toned-up muscle. Maybe she ought to do what her friend Ann was always suggesting, and go to some classes in self-defence.

But I never expected to have to defend myself against *Hugh*, she argued as she stepped out of the shower and began to dry herself with a huge fluffy towel. I thought he loved me. And then, with a tiny shock, I thought I loved him. . . .

Soberly, she went through to the bedroom. Like the rest of her flat, it was furnished in tones of cream, palest beige and soft gold. It was an environment that soothed her, made her feel calm and secure, but somehow tonight it gave her less comfort than usual. She wrapped a long silky housecoat around her and moved over to the dressing-table to dry her hair. Dark blue eyes, as troubled as a storm-driven lake, stared out of the mirror from a face that was paler than usual, its creaminess blanched to ivory. Damn Hugh, she thought, switching on her dryer and brushing her hair under the warm air. Damn *all* men.

But it wasn't really Hugh's fault, was it? Any more than it had been Richard's, when he'd proposed and been refused.

The truth was that this had happened all too often. Hugh had been nearer the mark than he'd known when he'd accused her of leading men on to the point of proposal and then turning them down. Only he hadn't been right about her motives. She *didn't* get any fun out of it—she *wasn't* a tease.

So what was she, then?

Verity laid down her brush and stared at her reflection. There had to be an answer. There had to be a reason why she did this—why she genuinely believed herself to be in love with each man, only to draw back almost in repugnance when he produced an engagement ring, as Hugh had done a few evenings ago. You couldn't blame him for being upset, she thought sadly. It had been a beautiful ring—a sapphire, to match her eyes—obviously expensive and chosen with some care. As evidence of his feelings, shouldn't it have been enough?

But it wasn't his feelings that were in doubt. And she knew that he would have made a good husband—faithful, prosperous, caring, everything that a husband should be, even if a little dull. And dullness wasn't a crime—was it?

It wasn't something that was common to all her men friends, either. Geoff certainly hadn't been dull, neither had Richard. Yet her reaction had been exactly the same when they'd proposed—an almost panic-stricken drawing back, the instinctive reaction of a wild animal when cornered by a predator.

So why? What was the reason?

Verity went on brushing her hair, watching absently as it changed from dark, tawny auburn to soft dawn-gold. Clearly it was something in her, nothing to do with the men who fell in love with her. And, equally clearly, she was going to have to find out what it was and do something about it before she dared embark on another relationship. She couldn't go on through life, building up her own hopes and those of each new man and then crashing them to the ground.

Because it was as disappointing for her as it was for them. She'd *wanted* to marry Hugh. And Richard. Or she'd thought she had.

Her hair dry now, Verity got up and wandered out through the living-room to the tiny, all-white kitchen to make herself a drink. Pouring hot milk into a pottery mug, she carried it back, settled herself into a corner of the big, cream-covered sofa and stared unseeingly at the picture over the fireplace.

There wasn't really any question about it, was there? She knew—if she were honest—just what the reason was for her not being able to marry any of the men who had asked her. Or any man at all—except for one.

A soft groan escaped Verity's lips as she fought with herself to face the truth. It was a truth she had pushed away, ignored, tried her hardest to deny. But it couldn't be denied any longer. If she were ever to find happiness, if she were ever to stop hurting other people, it had to be taken out of the dark cupboard of her mind, turned over and examined. It was unfinished business, and until it could be filed away marked 'closed' she would never be able to go ahead with her own life.

However much it might hurt, she had to open up that locked door, face up to what had happened five years ago and do something about it.

It was lucky, she thought as she went through the motions of arranging to be away, letting editors know that she meant to take a few months' sabbatical, asking a neighbour to keep an eye on her plants and send on any post, that the cottage was empty at the moment. It gave her a base; somewhere to stay, a place where she could be private and independent. Maybe something like this had been at the back of her mind all the time, preventing her from taking the final step of selling it.

Verity had moved down to Gloucestershire with her father just after leaving school. His illness, gradually creeping up on him for years, had reached a stage by then which meant that he was no longer able to work, and his only wish had been to leave the bustle of the city for the leafy countryside of his youth. With his elder daughter Sophie already a successful model, spending most of her time travelling, it had fallen to Verity to go with him. Not that he'd insisted on it— he'd stressed that he was quite happy to manage alone for as long as he was able, and could afford living-in help when it became essential. But Verity had refused to consider the idea. She could do her secretarial training at the college only fifteen miles away, she'd declared, and there was a good train service to take her in every morning and bring her home at night. They would have evenings and weekends together, and she could give him his breakfast in the morning and leave some lunch ready. There would be no problem at all.

And the cottage had been a success. Her father's last few months had been happy. She could never regret having given him those—even if her own experience had been rather more bitter. . . .

It was less than a week after moving in to Lane End that Verity had met Struan Courtney. And she'd had no premonition at all, when she first encountered him crossing the field behind the cottage, that he was to have such a drastic effect on her life. All the same, she'd been quite unable to avoid a catch in her breath when she saw him approaching with the easy, sinuous grace that she later recognised as characteristic of all his movements. And when he came nearer and impaled her with a glance from his light grey eyes, she'd found herself suddenly shivering.

There was something about him—an aura—that both scared and attracted her. It was as if beneath that bronzed skin and that thick black hair there was a dynamo rather than ordinary human bone and muscle. And there was something else—some reaction in him that he had immediately concealed, a reaction she didn't understand but translated as dislike. She gave an involuntary glance over her shoulder, wondering whether to turn and go back home. But that would be ridiculous. She was crossing by a public footpath, on her way to the village, and why should she let this stranger—whoever he was—stop her?

'You're Miss Sandison,' he stated, looking down at her. 'You've just moved into Lane End.'

'Yes, that's right.' To her annoyance, her voice wasn't much more than a whisper. 'I'm just going to the village—I'm living here with my father, he's an invalid and——'

'Yes, I'd heard.' A strange intentness darkened his silvery eyes. 'I ought to apologise—I meant to call in and see you both before this, but——' He broke off, noticing her puzzled expression, and added, 'I'm Struan Courtney. You bought the cottage from my brother, Justin.'

'Oh—oh yes.' Neither Verity nor her father had met the vendor of Lane End, the whole transaction having taken place through estate agents and solicitors. 'I thought it was from an estate,' she added.

'That's right, the Courtney Estate. You probably haven't lived here long enough yet to know that almost the whole village and quite a lot of the farms in the neighbourhood are owned by the estate.' There was a grimness in his voice she didn't properly understand. 'My brother owns the estate now, but he doesn't spend a lot of time here and I do most of the work of running it.' He stopped abruptly, as if he'd said too much, then went on with polite formality, 'And how are you settling in?'

'Oh, very well, thank you.' Verity shifted her basket on her arm, wishing that she knew how to say goodbye and go on her way without seeming rude. But she'd never seemed able to acquire the easy poise of her sister Sophie. Sophie wouldn't have had any trouble at all—but then, Sophie wouldn't have wanted to cut the conversation short. There was no denying it, Struan Courtney was a breathtakingly attractive man. And it wasn't just the dark hair that waved loosely over his broad forehead, or the straight line of his nose or the firmness of his lips. It wasn't his shoulders either, their muscularity evident under the dark blue shirt he wore, or the glimpse of dark hair exposed by the open neck. It wasn't any of these things—not entirely. It was something about the way he stood there, the expression in his eyes, the pull of a smile at his mouth, something Verity couldn't name but could recognise. Something she'd never found in any of the boyfriends she'd had at school. But then, they'd been just that—boys. Struan Courtney was, most definitely, a man...

She realised suddenly that she'd been staring at him, and felt her face flame with colour as she looked away from eyes that were again disturbingly intent. What was going on behind that broad, high forehead, she wondered, feeling mesmerised as she glanced back again to find him still watching her. And what on earth could he find so interesting in a rather shy and certainly not beautiful girl who must be at least ten or twelve years his junior? Why, to him she must seem no more than a child, the schoolgirl she'd so recently been. She tried to find that thought reassuring, but instead found herself oddly deflated.

'I feel I ought to say something traditional, meeting you like this,' he said solemnly, but with a hint of a smile in his voice. 'Like—are there any more at home like you?'

It hadn't been offered as a straw, but Verity grasped at it thankfully. 'Not like me, no,' she said, finding a smile from somewhere and wondering just why her voice still refused to behave properly. 'My sister Sophie is much more interesting. She's a model—she's not at home now, she has to travel a lot. I'm sure you've seen her picture, though. We're supposed to be alike,' she added ruefully, 'but I'm really just a poor imitation.'

'Nonsense!' The word was more like a bark, and Verity jumped, recoiling like a snail which has just put out a tentative stalk and had it roughly knocked back in. 'Don't disparage yourself,' Struan Courtney went on. 'Of course you're interesting—you're interesting to yourself, aren't you? Life isn't just a desert, it's opening up ahead of you, exciting and full of promise. Don't you feel that?' He waited for Verity's dumb nod. 'Well then—what makes you think you can't be interesting to anyone else?'

Completely taken aback, Verity looked at him more closely. She realised that her first impression had been of a man who was entirely self-contained in the way that a cat is self-contained, acutely sensitive to the world inasmuch as it affected himself. But now she realised that there was a deeper, more profound sensitivity in the line of his firm lips, the tilt of his light grey eyes and the planes of his cheeks. His words were abrupt, but they were sincere. He genuinely meant what he said.

'I—I suppose it's because I haven't had much time to do anything interesting,' she said at last. 'I only left school a few weeks ago. I haven't been anywhere, done anything. Sophie's been to——'

'For God's sake, there you go again,' he interrupted roughly. 'It's *you* I'm asking about, not Sophie. I've never even met your sister, and I'm sure I wouldn't recognise her—I never look at women's magazines, which is where I presume she figures most. All right, so you haven't been anywhere or done anything— presumably you don't intend that state of affairs to last. You mean your life to go on from here.'

What *was* the matter with him? He sounded almost angry with her—as if she'd done something deliberately to annoy him. Yet ten minutes ago he'd barely known of her existence. What could it matter to him how she saw her life?

'Well?' Struan said impatiently, and Verity realised that he was waiting for an answer and hastily gathered her wits together to give it to him.

'I'm going to secretarial college,' she told him hesitantly, and wondered whether to go on and tell him her real ambition—to be a journalist. Most people looked incredulous when she told them, warning her that she would have to learn to talk to people, rid herself of her almost incapacitating shyness. That was something Verity was painfully aware of, but it didn't prevent her ambition, or her determination to achieve it.

Struan said nothing for a moment, and she felt he was dismissing her as just another typist, filling in time before getting married. There were still girls who thought that way, she knew, but she wasn't one of them. She had never told anyone quite how deep her ambition went. Yet suddenly she had a feeling that she could have told Struan, that this stranger who seemed so vibrantly, almost dangerously, alive would in some odd way understand.

'I'll walk into the village with you,' he said abruptly, and as Verity could think of no way to dissuade him she found herself walking by his side through the grass. Only now did she realise the full extent of the tension that had built up between them, and she was relieved when Struan lessened it by talking in a desultory way about the countryside and asking her about her father.

'It sounds as if he's going to need quite a lot of nursing as time goes on,' he commented, when Verity had told him about the illness that had turned her father from a strong, active man to a near-invalid. 'Is that going to fall to you?'

'I don't mind,' she assured him quickly. 'After all, Dad took care of us after our mother died, which was when I was only two. It couldn't have been easy for him, but he coped and never complained. So now it's my turn.'

'And Sophie's,' Struan said quietly. Verity bit her lip. This was a thought that she didn't allow.

'Sophie had her career before Dad got sick. It would be crazy to make her give it up—not while I'm still at home. And when I've finished my training, I can still be around.' As a journalist? her mind mocked. But that was another thought which had to be pushed firmly away. There was freelancing, wasn't there? Anyway, it wasn't something she could think about yet—not until she'd done her secretarial course. And by then things

might be different—Sophie might be ready to come
home. Or——

They paused at a stile and Struan climbed over,
turning to offer Verity a hand. She could quite easily
have climbed over herself, without assistance, but the
gesture pleased her and she smiled at him and laid her
hand in his, letting her weight rest lightly against him.
And immediately stiffened.

His touch seared her like a heated brand. She gasped
and shrank away, but his fingers tightened round hers
and he drew her down from the stile, close against him.
His silvery eyes were very close to her face, their pupils
widening to night-dark pools, as if he had been
suddenly astounded. Verity could feel his warm breath
on her cheek. She wanted to look away but couldn't.
She was conscious of nothing in those few whirling
seconds, nothing other than Struan's closeness, the
mesmeric quality of his eyes, the long fingers that were
still wound round her own, and a sudden unbelievable
sense of recognition.

And then Struan let go of her hand and moved
away, his expression unreadable. Verity let out the
breath she hadn't realised she'd been holding. Shakily,
she held out her hand for the basket she had given
Struan as she climbed the stile, and he gave it back to
her.

'There's a weak place in that hedge,' he remarked, his
voice abstracted as if he wasn't really thinking about
what he was saying. 'I'll have to get someone to look at
that ...' His voice drifted away, and Verity had the
impression that he was talking at random. Tentatively,
she turned her head to look at him. He met her eyes,
but his own were veiled, unreadable. And as they began
to walk again, she noticed that he kept himself slightly
apart, almost as if he were afraid of the effect of any
accidental contact between them. The tension was there

again, as vibrant as electricity, and Verity hadn't the least idea what to do about it.

Sophie would have known. But Sophie was four years older, and even as a child had possessed a sophistication that Verity lacked. And whatever Struan Courtney might say, Verity was sure that he would find her sister much more to his taste than this shy, gauche schoolgirl who walked beside him now. Struan Courtney might spend his life running a country estate, but he was no country bumpkin, and Verity felt quite certain that he would be as much at home at the parties and nightclubs that Sophie's world knew as he was here, striding across the fields.

That moment of electric attraction, that brief recognition, meant nothing. And once Struan had made his courtesy call at Lane End, she was unlikely to see anything more of him.

But in that Verity was wrong. Over the next few months, Struan called often at the cottage. He got on well with John Sandison and the two would spend hours talking. It became a habit for Verity to walk across the fields with him afterwards, and from that it was a natural progression to having the odd day out together, the three of them. Verity found herself relaxing in Struan's company, losing that paralysing shyness, discovering a talent for conversation which she had never suspected. It still seemed astonishing to her that her thoughts, her opinions, should be worth listening to, her quips found amusing. And yet Struan seemed to think they were, and she felt a warm gratitude towards him for the confidence that was growing in her.

'You know, you ought to learn to drive,' he told her one day as they sauntered up the sloping meadow behind Lane End. 'You could take your father out yourself then, instead of having to rely on the few spare days I can afford.'

Verity immediately felt cold. Was he telling her he was tired of transporting them around? She looked at him, and her widening eyes must have expressed something of her feelings, for he stopped and laid his hands on her shoulders.

'Don't look at me like that! You make me feel——' He didn't go on, but his own eyes were darkening, and once again she felt the electric shiver that always came with his touch. Neither of them had ever mentioned it, but she knew by his reaction that he felt it too. Normally, he moved away as if he'd been stung. But this time he didn't. He stayed there, his hands burning through the thin cotton of her shirt, his eyes almost black.

'You don't have to spend so much time with us,' she whispered, although she knew both mind and body wanted to say something very different. 'We—we're very grateful, but you honestly don't——'

'Stop it!' His voice was ragged and he caught her against him, jerking her almost off her feet so that she came into violent contact with the hardness of his body. 'Don't talk to me like that about gratitude! You've nothing to be grateful for, nothing, do you hear me?' He stared down at her, eyes like burning coals, jaw tense. 'Everything I've done over these past months has been done because *I* wanted it—understand? Because I wanted to see your father—I like him, I count him as one of my friends. And——' his voice softened, became little more than a husky murmur '—because I wanted to see you.'

Verity stood quite still. She was acutely aware of his body, pressed firmly against hers, aware of the beat of his heart against her breast, aware of the wild pounding of her own. He couldn't be saying these

things, she thought dazedly. Not to her. It couldn't be
happening.

And then shock tore at her as Struan raised one hand
to her chin, lifting it with a finger. He looked long and
deep into her eyes, and there was no way she could look
away. In the end, she could tolerate it no longer. She let
her lids droop, hiding the terror. And the next second
his lips were on hers and she was held fast in an iron
grip against a body that felt like steel, yet had a curious,
exciting resilience. Her mouth was being teased and
opened by lips that acknowledged no refusal, by a
tongue that probed the softness with a gentle yet
inexorable insistence. The pounding of her heart
increased until she was dimly afraid that it would burst,
and there was a roaring in her ears which blotted out all
the sounds she had been aware of before. There was
nothing in the world any more but Struan—his body,
his hands, his kiss.

For the first few whirling seconds Verity stood rigid,
too startled to react in any way. Then, instinctively, she
moved to pull away, her inexperience rebelling against
this unexpected invasion. But Struan merely tightened his
arms about her. And then her own body took over, and a
response as old as time swept her into a storm of emotion
that took her entirely by surprise. Yet it was as if she had
always known this would happen, always known that one
day Struan would hold her and kiss her in just such a way,
always known that she would respond—be impelled to
respond—with a passionate fervour that had her weak
and shaking in his arms, her mouth seeking his, her
tongue exploring, experimenting, her body moving
with a new sensuality against his hardness.

At last Struan released her. His arms relaxed round
her, his mouth lifted from hers, and when Verity
opened her eyes she found him looking down at her, his
eyes dark with tenderness, his mouth soft.

'I didn't mean that to happen yet,' he said quietly. 'I meant to wait—to give you more time. But I just couldn't help myself.' He touched her cheek with his fingertip, tracing a wondering line down to her slender neck. 'Should I be sorry?'

Verity shook her head speechlessly. 'I'm not sorry,' she whispered, and found that her arms were round his neck where they must have curled themselves at some point during that earth-shaking kiss. She let her palms slip down to rest lightly on his shoulders, feeling the hardness of his collarbone under her fingers. 'I'm very glad.'

Struan shook his head slightly, a smile coming into his eyes. 'You're a brazen hussy, you know that?' He bent his head and kissed her again, lightly this time, a brushing of his lips across hers that sent Verity's senses reeling again. 'You realise we're in full view of half the village here?'

It was an exaggeration, as Verity knew—only their cottage looked directly on to this meadow, and the more outlying houses that also had a view of it were too far away to be able to pick out any figures. But she smiled at Struan and allowed him to take her hand as they continued their climb. At the top of the hill there was a knot of pine trees that sang in the breeze; with a view of seven counties, you could still have complete privacy. Her heart kicked as she thought of what might happen when they reached it.

They were both breathless when they finally came to the summit, and Verity leaned against one of the trees, laughing as Struan came up to her. She turned her face, lifting it towards him, lips slightly parted in invitation. But instead of bending towards it he looked gravely at her, taking her hand and stroking it almost absently.

'I meant what I said, Verity,' he said at last as she stared at him, feeling suddenly anxious. 'I didn't mean that to happen yet. You—you're so damned young. And there are other things . . .' He bit his lip, frowning, and Verity had a sudden panic-stricken feeling that he was slipping away from her.

'I'm not that young!' she burst out. 'I'm nearly nineteen! Plenty of girls are earning their own living at my age, married even, with children——' She stopped suddenly, afraid that she had said too much. Suppose Struan thought that after one kiss she expected marriage! Her face was hot with colour and she looked at the ground. It was deep with scattered pine-needles, she noticed with detachment, and their scent was all around.

'Nearly nineteen, yes,' Struan repeated quietly. 'And I'm nearly thirty, Verity. That's a large gap, especially now. In another ten years, when you've lived a little, gained your own experience, it might not seem so much. But now——'

'And what experience do I need?' she asked desperately. 'I might stay here for those ten years, living with Dad, doing exactly what I do now. What experience would I have then that I don't have now? What difference would it make?'

He lifted his shoulders. 'We can't tell, can we?' His eyes were on hers, their silver a thin glittering rim round the darkness of his pupils. 'And we can't put the clock back, either. Maybe I was wrong to think we could even make it stand still. It's happened now. We can't go back to where we were before.'

Verity put her head against his chest, feeling the warm strength of it. 'I don't want to,' she whispered. 'I want to go on—to wherever we go next.' With an absolute certainty, she knew that it had to be somewhere good. This was meant to be, had been meant from the start. Nothing could go wrong with what was betweeen her and Struan.

'Let's sit down.' Struan spread his pullover on the brown carpet of pine-needles and drew her down beside him. He put his arm round her, and she rested against the bulwark of his shoulder. 'I don't know how much you know about my family, Verity—you must have heard quite a lot in the village, apart from what I've told you.'

Which hadn't been much, she thought—Struan was not given to talking at length about himself. 'I know that your family has lived here for generations,' she said, 'and that you run the estate for your brother Justin. But I don't know much more than that.'

'Well, there's not really much more to know. Not of any importance. As you've gathered, Justin is the heir and came into the estate when our father died a few years ago. Our mother was like yours—died when we were quite young, the main difference being that we were brought up by a nanny and were packed off to boarding school as soon as we were old enough. I didn't hate it—I tolerated it and lived for the holidays when I could come back to the estate. I spent all the time I could running round the farms, helping out wherever they'd let me, until I was old enough to be of some real use. Justin was different. He loved school because he found himself mixing with the kind of people he was at home with. He spent his holidays with his friends, cruising on their yachts, going to parties as he got older, seeing London. It was quite natural that when we left school he should go on doing that and I should learn to run the estate.'

'Even though you were never likely to inherit it?' Verity asked, and he shrugged.

'Why should that matter? Justin was keen for the place to do well, to be kept up in the traditional manner. So there would always be a place for an estate manager, and there was no reason why it shouldn't be

me. I love Courtneys,' he added quietly, gazing out at
the countryside that was spread at their feet. 'I wouldn't
want to live anywhere else.'

There was a short silence. Verity was conscious of a
deep happiness. She knew now that she had loved
Struan from that first moment when they had met,
down there in the meadow. She had been too
inexperienced, too uncertain of herself then to recognise
the emotion for what it was. She had sensed Struan's
virility and her own feminine response to it, and had
translated the first into arrogance and the second into
fear. Now, with several months between that day and
this, she could relax in the knowledge that she
understood the man Struan was—strong but sensitive,
dynamic yet tender. And perhaps he had felt the same—
recognised, at the identical moment, the bond there was
between them, but wisely decided to wait, to restrain
himself until she was ready.

Well, now she was ready. And it seemed a long time
since that first, shattering kiss.

She ought to have known, of course, that it couldn't
last. Happiness like that was too frail a bubble, too
shimmeringly exquisite, not to shatter. Sophie would
have known, she thought wryly. But then, Sophie
would never have taken it so seriously in the first place.
She would have seen it for what it was.

And that was——? Even now, five years later, Verity
could still not face up to the painful truth, still winced
away from it.

For a few weeks, she and Struan had shared an idyll.
They had said nothing to anyone else, though she
thought her father must have guessed. She would look
up sometimes from a book to find his eyes resting on
her as if in relief, a gentle happiness in his tired face. He
would welcome Struan with a new warmth, and he left

them alone more and more, saying that he needed to rest, that they ought to be out making the most of the late summer days. He was quietly insistent, so that Verity felt no guilt at leaving him alone, though she was uneasily aware that his health was failing more rapidly than the doctors had expected.

'It's the cold weather I'm afraid of,' Jamie Kenwood, the local doctor, told her one October morning when a frost rimed the bare branches of the trees. 'I've a feeling we're in for a hard winter, and it won't suit your father at all. He needs to get away somewhere warm. I suppose there isn't any chance . . .?'

'I'd do anything,' Verity had answered, her mind already clicking through the various possibilities. 'My sister knows some people who've got a villa in Portugal—would that be any good? I'm sure she's told me they don't intend to use it this winter—they're going to Australia to see relations. I could find out . . .'

'That would be ideal.' Jamie looked at her thoughtfully. 'But what about you? Aren't you doing a course at the college?'

'That doesn't matter—not when Dad's health is at stake. And I could probably carry it on by correspondence.' Verity stood up, anxious to contact Sophie and find out if the scheme were possible. 'I'll let you know as soon as we've got things arranged.'

It was only when she was outside Jamie's house, walking along the bright, cold lane back to the cottage, that she realised just what she was doing. Committing herself to months in a foreign country.

Months away from Struan.

But it would be all right, she assured herself, as soon as the first chill struck a spear into her heart. She would miss him, of course. There were times when she wouldn't know how to bear it, when she would ache for the feel of his arms around her, his kisses scorching her lips. But it wouldn't change anything between them. Nothing could do that. What they had was strong, enduring, a love that would last a lifetime, a love that nothing could destroy.

And afterwards, amidst all the bitterness and anguish, she had only been able to ask herself that one question, repeating it over and over again, and knowing there could never be any satisfactory answer.

How could she have been so naïve? How *could* she have been so naïve?

Because when she returned from Portugal alone, after her father's sudden death, it was to find that Struan wasn't there to comfort her, to take her in his arms and give her his strength, to kiss her back to life.

Instead, Struan Courtney was on the point of marriage—to Gina Brand.

CHAPTER TWO

I'M still not at all sure this was a good idea, Verity thought as she stopped her car by the side of the road and gazed out over the rolling meadows towards Courtneys.

Since Hugh's proposal a week ago, she had spent most of her time going over and over the events of five years earlier. It was pointless, she'd kept telling herself, yet she knew that the key to her problems still lay here, at Courtneys. It was still held in the hands of Struan Courtney, that dark, enigmatic man who had caught at her heart when she was barely eighteen and had never let it go.

Unfinished business, her friend Ann had agreed when Verity told her the whole story. You won't ever be free of him until you've seen him and laid the ghost. 'And that's probably all it is,' she'd added with a smile. 'It's my guess he's a settled family man now, with a couple of kids and a paunch, and you'll wonder what you ever saw in him.'

'I wish I could believe that,' Verity sighed. 'But I can't somehow see Struan Courtney running to seed. He was too—too vital, too alive.'

'And you were just eighteen,' Ann reminded her. 'Impressionable, unsophisticated, ripe for your first affair. Or, failing that, an infatuation. Honestly, Verity, that's all it was. How could it be anything else, in the circumstances?'

How indeed? A man of almost thirty and a girl of eighteen—how could it have been anything but infatuation? And yet—if that were really all it was, could it have lasted for five years, dormant in some corner of her heart, waking only in her dreams and when she received a proposal?

Verity shifted restlessly in the driving seat. Her Volvo was comfortable on even the longest drive, but somehow today nothing was right. It was nerves, she told herself with irritation, and it was crazy that in this day and age a liberated girl like herself, earning good money as a freelance journalist, should allow herself to get into such a state over a man she'd known five years earlier. Ann was right. It was 'unfinished business', nothing more, and the sooner she faced Struan again and saw for herself what he was really like the sooner she'd get him out of her system.

Taking one last look at the big Georgian house which lay dreaming on its knoll across the fields, Verity started the engine. She knew that she couldn't actually go seeking Struan out—he was married, after all, and she had no desire to become a home-wrecker. But she could go to the cottage, open it up again, perhaps try to find in its peaceful atmosphere something of the youthful, unbruised Verity who had lived here five years ago. Perhaps that would be enough; perhaps then, after a few months, she could put this behind her, go back to London and her busy life and start anew. Perhaps she didn't really need to see Struan at all.

And if she did bump into him—well, she would leave that to Fate to decide. Probably, as Ann said, he would have lost his charisma, his magnetism, and she would be able to laugh at herself and wonder whatever all the fuss was about.

And the memory of that last day, just before Struan's wedding, could be placed firmly where it belonged, in the past.

The shocks had begun before then, of course. There had

been her father's death, coming so unexpectedly when he had seemed to be so much better. At least it had been peaceful, taking him during his sleep, but that hadn't helped Verity when she had entered his room with his breakfast tray, already talking cheerfully about the outing they'd planned for that day. The stillness of the figure in the bed had stopped the words on her lips; slowly, she'd put down the tray and touched his face. It was quite cold.

The local English doctor and community had been overwhelmingly kind and helpful, taking all the burden of making arrangements out of Verity's hands, coping with it all. She'd let Struan know immediately, had even hoped that he might come to her. But his voice had sounded oddly distant on the crackling phone, and he hadn't said anything about coming to Portugal. She'd finished the call feeling blank and somewhat disturbed. Perhaps a letter would tell her more, she thought. But when it came it was short and almost formal, and she'd had a chilled premonition that her whole life was falling apart.

It was a feeling that had persisted through all the complications of returning home. Without a lot of hope, she wrote to Struan to tell him when she would arrive. Fortunately, Sophie's friends who owned the villa were able to help with a private flight to a small local airport, so she was spared the trauma of a complex journey, and landed on a cold February afternoon on an almost deserted airstrip only twenty miles away from home.

She came into the minute arrivals area, pulling her coat around her against the unaccustomed cold. Would Struan be here to meet her? Surely he must be—she remembered the way he'd held her when they'd said goodbye, the hint of desperation in his mouth as he'd kissed her for the last time. Did he know then that it was all going to go wrong, that when she returned he would be engaged to another girl? Was it a more final goodbye than she'd dreamed as she'd clung to him and wished she'd never agreed to go?

It seemed that it must have been, for Struan wasn't there to meet her, his dark hair blowing in the icy wind. Instead, her eyes lighted on another familiar figure, a man whose height wasn't much more than hers, whose brown hair was rough and untidy, but whose eyes were warm, friendly and concerned. He saw her at the same moment and came over with quick steps, and Verity caught his hand and kissed his cheek with relief that at least *someone* had come to meet her.

'Jamie! It was good of you to come.'

'I had to. I feel responsible—after all, it was my idea that you should go to Portugal.' His brown eyes looked her over. 'You've had an unhappy time, Verity, and I'm sorry,' he said quietly. 'If I'd had any idea it would end this way——'

'Don't be silly,' she broke in. 'No one could have known what would happen. And Dad enjoyed those last few months. He seemed—I really thought he was better, you know——' Her voice broke, and then she steadied it and went on, 'I'm glad we went. And I'm glad it was that way—quick, before his illness made him completely helpless. He dreaded that.'

'Yes, you're right. It was better this way.' He led her to where his car was waiting and settled her into it. 'We'll go and have some tea, and then I'll take you home. You must be exhausted.'

She was, but there were things she had to know before they went to Lane End, and she was glad of the chance to ask Jamie. He would know what had happened to Struan, surely—for *something* must have happened to stop those long, funny, passionate letters that she'd been accustomed to receive every few days.

Something must have happened to make him sound so
distant on the phone, to make him write so formally
after her father's death. And Jamie, who was one of
Struan's closest friends, would know.

The question was—would he tell her? Verity wished
now that they hadn't kept their love so secret, feeling
that it was too precious as yet to share. If Jamie knew
they'd been in love, their understanding so complete
that it didn't need words, he would have told her
straight away. As it was—well, she'd have to be
discreet.

'Tell me all the latest gossip, then,' she suggested
when they were sitting over tea by a log fire in a nearby
hotel. 'What's been happening since I've been away?
Any matches, hatches or despatches?' She kept her tone
light, but couldn't prevent a slight quiver as she asked
the last question.

'The usual amount of all three,' he said, but there was
a gravity in his tone that caused her to look sharply at
him. 'One or two of the older people succumbed to the
winter, as one might expect, but I don't think you knew
them. A couple of new babies to take their place, down
on the council estate. And—well, I don't suppose you
heard about Justin, did you?'

'Justin? Justin Courtney?' Verity jerked her head up
to stare at him. 'Struan's brother? No, I never heard a
thing—what's happened to him?'

'Killed in a crash in a light aircraft,' Jamie told her
laconically. 'Happened a few weeks ago. Flying was his
latest craze—you know what he was like, the complete
playboy, jetting around the world, figuring in all the
best gossip columns.' His tone was dry. 'He didn't often
put in an appearance at Courtneys, and I think the
locals had almost forgotten he actually owned the place.
Tragic, of course, but it hasn't actually changed
anything—the estate now belongs to Struan, which is

popular enough with everyone, and nothing's really any different.'

He paused while Verity took in this new information. So that's why Struan had become so remote—with his brother dying, he must have had a million things to do; even if Justin hadn't often come to Courtneys there must have been legalities to go through, documents to draft and sign—she didn't really know what it would involve, but it was surely adequate excuse for not finding time to write letters. But why hadn't he told her? Hadn't he wanted support, just as she'd wanted it when her father died? And hard on the heels of that thought came the answer. Struan had known her father was ill—he hadn't wanted to worry her with his own concerns. There would be time enough to tell her the new situation when she returned.

Which still left her with one question—why hadn't he come to meet her?

'That's except for one thing,' she heard Jamie saying, and jerked her mind back to attention.

'Except for one thing?'

'One thing different. For Struan.' Jamie chose a cake, evidently unaware of Verity's sudden tension as she stared at him. 'You've come back at a good time, Verity,' he continued cheerfully. 'You'll be able to attend the wedding. Everyone's invited, and you were quite friendly with Struan yourself, weren't you? I daresay your invitation is sitting on your doormat right now, waiting for you to open it.'

'Invitation?' she managed to say through lips that were suddenly dry. 'Wedding? Jamie, I don't know what you're talking about.'

'Why, Struan's wedding, of course. It's on Saturday.' Jamie glanced up and caught sight of her face. 'Yes, it came as a surprise to us too,' he said, wiping his fingers. 'Nobody even knew he was contemplating marriage, and Gina had never been down here before. But Struan was never one to bow to convention, and if he decided that this was the right time to get married, that would be it. It's been arranged in rather a rush—a whirlwind romance, I suppose you'd call it—but it's time Struan married, and I suppose what happened to Justin made him decide not to wait. Estates like this need heirs, you see. There's an entail on this one—it always has to go to a son, and if there isn't a son it goes to another branch of the family.'

'That's rather hard on daughters,' Verity said, one part of her amazed that she could still carry on a normal conversation while the rest of her felt that it was dying.

Jamie smiled. 'It is, but entails were drawn up before Women's Lib came on the scene. Daughters don't do too badly—there's a trust income which is still quite generous. But naturally the present incumbent is always keen to provide himself with a son or two, to make sure of the succession. Quite a few people were beginning to feel that Justin was leaving it rather late, I know.'

Verity suddenly found the conversation distasteful. All this talk of entails, heirs, inheritances—what did it have to do with the love she'd shared with Struan? She remembered that first morning, meeting on the field path, the day they'd climbed the hill behind the cottage and Struan had kissed her under the singing pines. Had it all been a dream, a fantasy, or—worse still—a lie? Had she misunderstood everything that Struan had said? Had she been a gullible fool, taken in by a smooth tongue and a pair of silvery eyes?

'Can we go now, Jamie?' she asked, reaching for her bag and jacket. 'I'm rather tired—I'd just like to be back at the cottage. Do you mind?'

'Of course not!' He was on his feet, looking down at her with concern in his brown eyes. 'You do look rather shattered, Verity—I hadn't realised. It's been a difficult time for you.' He took her hand, holding it gently. 'Look—you won't mind if I call in and see you occasionally, will you? You don't know many people in the village. I want you to feel that you've got one friend to call on.'

Verity looked at him and felt her eyes mist over. It was such a different homecoming from what she had expected. She had seen herself so many times, throwing herself into Struan's arms, resting in the circle of his embrace as if she had come into a safe harbour. And, instead, there was no Struan, nor could there ever be again. She didn't know what had happened—and she had a feeling she would never know, for surely Struan wouldn't seek her out, and she couldn't risk any further hurt by going to confront him. It was over, as certainly as her father's life was over, and she didn't really know how she was going to bear it.

'Thank you Jamie,' she said, letting her hand stay in his. 'It's good to know you're my friend.'

Of course, she hadn't been able to avoid meeting Struan. For one thing there was the invitation, waiting as Jamie had said it would be. She drew it out of its envelope and stared at it, taking in the silver deckled edge, the flowing italic script that invited her to the wedding of Virginia Brand to Struan John Courtney at the local church on Saturday afternoon. Reception to be held at Courtney Grange.

Why there? she wondered dully, and then noticed that the wording on the card was unusual—there was no mention of Gina's parents, and the invitation seemed to have come from the bride and groom themselves. Perhaps Gina had no family, or perhaps they lived abroad. Or perhaps they simply didn't approve of this rushed wedding.

But was it really so rushed? Nobody had known about Gina, Jamie had said—yet nobody had known about Verity either. Struan was evidently good at keeping secrets; maybe he'd been seeing Gina for a lot longer than anyone supposed—even while he was seeing Verity. Maybe, on the evenings when he hadn't been with her, he'd been with Gina Brand, planning their wedding, laughing over the simple eighteen-year-old who provided him with a little amusement on the side. Although it wasn't likely that Gina had known about Verity—not many brides would have stood for even such ineffectual competition as she had been.

The first shock had worn off, and now a bitter anger was beginning to smoulder deep down inside Verity. She stared at the invitation again, then ripped it across from side to side, again and again until it was in shreds. With swift, jerky movements, she crossed to the fireplace and dropped it on the logs piled there. Then she took a box of matches from the mantelpiece and knelt to set light to them.

And as she watched the flames leap up the chimney, it seemed to her that the last of her childhood was going with them. From now on, she was truly a woman.

Her second ordeal came two days later, when she went to the village for some shopping and met Struan.

It had been bad enough, she thought, having to answer everyone's enquiries about her father, bad enough to accept their commiserations, kindly meant though they were. Any bereaved person must feel the same, she thought—that first, harrowing trip back into the world, when each person you spoke to felt that something must be said yet didn't know what. So few people could offer condolences without stumbling over their own embarrassment, and the more they said the worse it was. Verity found that she preferred the simple 'I'm so sorry' to the more gushing sentimentalising, and resolved to remember that for when she met someone in a similar situation.

Her chance came sooner than she expected. Rounding the last corner before taking the field path, she found herself face to face with Struan. She stopped at once, crushing down her first impulse to turn tail and run, and looked up at him as steadily as she could. And realised that he too had changed.

He was thinner, his face almost haggard, his eyes haunted. There was something—some expression—that she didn't understand. A flicker as he looked at her, something that could have been an appeal for understanding but which vanished before she could catch it. And then nothing but a remoteness that turned him into a stranger.

There was no way for Verity to pass him; he seemed to fill the narrow track leading to the stile. It was the stile where he'd first held her, she remembered bleakly, just after she'd moved here with her father. The thought brought an added shaft of pain, and then she remembered that he'd lost someone too since then.

'I was sorry to hear about your brother,' she said quietly, and he nodded.

'I didn't write a very adequate letter after your father died—I hope you'll forgive me.' His voice was toneless. He gestured slightly with his hand. 'There were things . . .'

'Yes.' Verity was silent. Just what things did he mean—the legal complications of Justin's death, or his relationship with Gina? She wished bitterly, as she'd wished a thousand times, that she hadn't come back just now, only days before his wedding. She supposed she'd have to mention it—but what could she say? If only he would let her pass—but he showed no signs of moving.

'You received my invitation?' He bit the words out

and she flinched away from the harshness of his tone. What was the matter with him? He had no reason to be angry with *her*. She lifted her chin, conscious of a sudden spurt of anger of her own.

'Yes. I shan't be coming, of course.'

'Oh?' He couldn't be surprised, but neither surely could he be quite so indifferent as he sounded. 'Why's that? Another engagement?'

Verity stared at him and her control snapped. How could he stand there, so coolly arrogant, and ask her why she wasn't coming to his wedding? Had he really forgotten everything? Had he forgotten the passion that had flared betweeen them in this very lane, on the hilltop that rose above them, in so many hidden places? Had he forgotten that last night, when they'd clung to each other and whispered words of love—words that Verity had meant with all her being, words that she'd believed he meant with equal sincerity?

'No, I haven't got another engagement—now!' she snapped, and was gratified to see a flicker of emotion in his eyes—eyes that today were the grey of pewter. 'But I thought I had one. An engagement with you, even though we never made it official.' Her own eyes filled with tears as she stared at him, the bitterness of her pain like a knife in her heart. 'Struan, how could you do it? How could you treat me like this? We had something good and precious, and now—now you've smirched it, you've turned it into something squalid and petty. What happened? Why did you forget me?'

Struan's eyes were veiled, as expressionless as stones, his face closed. He looked down at her without emotion and she knew with frightening certainty that something had happened to him while she was away, something that had taken him beyond her reach. But what could it be?

'You're obviously still upset, Verity,' he said coldly.

'It's understandable—you've worked hard, looking after your father and trying to hold down your course at the same time. And now you're on your own, it's natural that you should still be feeling overwrought. Can't your sister help? Perhaps you could go to her for a while. It must have brought back old memories, coming back here.'

Verity stared at him. 'Yes, it has—memories that you would obviously prefer I forgot! Struan, what's happened? Can't you at least be honest with me?' Again, she thought she caught that flicker of feeling, but it was gone at once. 'Struan, you told me—I thought——' She floundered, then told herself that the words had to be said. 'I thought you loved me,' she said, facing him squarely. 'I thought you wanted to marry me.'

There was a moment's complete silence. Then Struan moved his shoulders slightly and Verity knew that she had lost. Not that there'd ever been any hope of anything else, she realised. And looking at that cold, implacable face, she began to wonder why she'd ever loved him at all.

'I'm sorry, Verity,' he said then, his voice quiet. 'You obviously read a great deal more into what was nothing more than a casual friendship than I meant you to. Oh, I admit we had fun—you're a nice kid and I enjoyed being with you. And I got the impression that you enjoyed finding out a bit about life from me. But that's all it was, and I'm sorry if I gave you the impression it was anything more. I certainly didn't mean to.'

Verity stood before him, shaking her head slowly. It wasn't true—none of it was true. He *had* loved her—she was ready to swear he'd loved her. All right, so it hadn't lasted and now he'd fallen in love with someone else, but that didn't wipe out what had happened between them. It didn't make it any less true.

Struan's expression changed again as he looked at her, and she got the impression that his control was tightly stretched over emotions that he dared not release. Suppose she tested him? Suppose she tried to find out what it was that lay beneath the surface, seething under the icy exterior?

Parting her lips slightly, she stepped forward and laid her hands on his shoulders in the way that she'd learned he liked. She lifted her face to his and let the tip of her tongue wet her lips.

'All right, Struan,' she whispered. 'It was a bit of fun—nothing more than that. So what about a kiss for old times' sake?'

For a moment, she thought he was going to refuse her challenge. And then, with a muffled groan, he took her by the shoulders and laid his mouth briefly on hers.

His touch was light, a butterfly contact only, yet it burned into Verity's skin like hot iron. A spiral of tingling sensation uncoiled somewhere low in her stomach and weakness invaded her. When Struan led her round the corner into the dark shadow of an old stone wall, she leaned against it, thankful for its rough support. Her breath was coming with difficulty.

'Oh, God,' he said with a groan, 'why did you have to do that, Verity? Why?' And as she stared up at him in terror, he bent his head and laid his lips on her mouth again.

Verity gasped, and a tiny whimper came into her throat. Somehow, in the past few months and especially in the last day, she had forgotten the storm of emotion Struan could arouse in her, forgotten the tempest that could blaze between them both at a touch. Briefly, she regretted having issued that challenge—but it was too late now, and she knew that unless Struan chose otherwise there was only one inevitable outcome. And it couldn't happen like this—it mustn't—he was getting *married* in two days' time—she must stop him! But she was helpless as he slid his arms round her and gathered her close, the soft touch of his lips like silk against hers. Somewhere behind the softness, she knew, there was a dynamic tension that could find expression in only one way, a passion that could barely be repressed.

Terror warred with her own driving response—her body was clamouring for release, and she was desperately afraid that she wouldn't be able to control it. And even as she thought this with the one part of her mind that was still dimly working, she felt a deep groan vibrate somewhere low in Struan's broad chest. It was a groan that seemed to act like a catalyst on them both, so that as he pulled her even more tightly against him she found that her own hands were gripping his shoulders, winding up round his neck, tangling in his thick black hair. Instinctively, she let her mouth open under the increased pressure of his lips, and a surge of desire swept through her as his tongue took immediate and joyous advantage, forcing itself between her teeth, exploring each warm, moist crevice. At the same time one of his hands began to caress her body, each circling movement becoming more intimate as his other arm held Verity in a firm grasp which was all that kept her upright.

When he finally removed his mouth from hers, she was drooping across his arm, powerless to resist him. Her own passion was implicit in the rapid breathing that made her breasts rise and fall against him, her back slightly arched so that the tender curves were strained against the thin wool of the pullover she wore under her jacket, unbuttoned now by Struan's impatient fingers. Slowly, as if drugged, she opened her eyes and stared at him, catching the expression of hunger as he looked down and let his fingers stray lightly down the neckline,

passing the shirt she wore beneath the pullover and into
the hidden shadows of the cleft beneath.

'My God,' he muttered, and bent his head again to
lay a kiss between her breasts. 'My God, what's
happened to me?'

His words brought Verity back to life. Desire was
replaced by horror as she struggled to regain her
balance, but to do so she had to hold on to his
shoulders again, and for a moment they were both
almost swept away once more. But now Struan had
regained command of himself. He held Verity upright, still
keeping his hands on her arms, still holding her close—
too close, she thought in agony—but looking at her
now with a sombreness that was almost frightening.

'I suppose you won't believe me if I say I didn't
intend that to happen,' he said, his voice tight with the
control he was exercising over it.

Verity couldn't speak. She gazed up at him, begging
him speechlessly to let her go. If he understood her
message, he ignored it.

'Why in hell should this happen now?' he asked,
lifting his face so that he seemed to be addressing the
sky. 'Why should it happen at all? I swore——' He
stopped abruptly, coming back to stare intently down
into Verity's pale face. He lifted one hand, laid his
finger under her chin, turning her face this way and that
as if he wanted to study its every angle by the light of
the pale February sun. 'You—an awkward, inexperienced little teenager—a good ten years younger than I
am, you've done nothing, seen nothing, you aren't even
grown up yet. Why, for God's sake, do you have to
have *this* effect on me? And what the hell can I do
about it?'

Verity stared up at his tortured face, its lines made
harsher, older by the darkness. Her heart was
thundering, her legs shaking. She wished she had never

met Struan—wished she had never come to Lane End. She was terrified in case he began to kiss her again, knowing that she would be powerless to stop him—yet at the same time she longed to be back in his arms, tasting the joyous rapture that they'd known before she went away. And at the back of every thought was Gina—Struan's fiancée. Struan's bride.

'Please,' she said feebly, 'you mustn't . . . Please, let me go.'

'Let you go,' he said on a groan. 'I know that's what I've got to do.' His passion broke through again, bringing angry frustration to his voice. 'You should never have come back here, Verity,' he said roughly, stepping away from her. 'You should have kept well away from me. Or, having come back you should have made very sure that we didn't meet again.' His eyes were stormy as he stared down at her, and she quailed before the dark emotion that stirred their depths like an unnamed monster in a lake. 'But don't make any mistake about it,' he went on harshly, 'it's nothing but a physical thing that's between us. All right, I find you attractive—I can't deny it, can I? There's something in you that calls out to me, and when you're near me it almost drives me wild with wanting . . . But that's all there is to it, and all there ever could have been.' He turned away abruptly. as if he couldn't bear to be near her any longer, then twisted back, and she cringed away from the ravaged look on his face. 'Keep right away from me in future, Verity,' he ground out. 'Keep right away. It's the only answer for both of us.'

He let her go then, watching her climb the stile with a shakiness that he didn't attempt to help. She was glad he didn't: his touch might have set them both alight, and the thought of it was pure terror. Blindly, she stumbled across the field, letting herself into the cottage as if she were reaching sanctuary. Blindly, she found her

way across the kitchen to the table and sank down on a
chair, her arms spread across the old, scrubbed pine.

She had expected that the tears would come then. But
they didn't. Maybe she'd already cried too many.

And she was still dry-eyed when, two days later, she
heard the church bells ringing and knew that Struan
Courtney was marrying Gina Brand just across the
meadow.

CHAPTER THREE

VERITY brought her car to a stop at the end of the lane and sat for a moment, gazing at the tangled garden of the cottage. It was exactly as she remembered it—almost as if it had stayed frozen in time, while the world went on without it. The same rioting garden, filled with the soft colours of lavender, love-in-a-mist, love-lies-bleeding—the old-fashioned flowers with their evocative names. The same shabby thatch on the roof—a little more worn now, perhaps, and in need of repair. The same nests under the eaves, with house-martins flying back and forth feeding their voracious young. Quite possibly the very same birds, she thought, remembering that martins always returned to the same spot, year after year.

It might be quite nice to be a house-martin, she reflected ruefully. At least they made faithful partners. But it was she who had flown away, wasn't it—only to find that there was, after all, no nest to return to, no partner to welcome her back.

She felt again the surge of pain, and wondered whether it had really been wise to come back here, scene of so much happiness and so much anguish. But if ever she were to exorcise the ghost of her love for Struan, the ghost that was holding her back from life, it had to be here. And she hoped the place would be enough. Walking in the fields where she'd strolled with Struan, climbing the hill where they'd first kissed, revisiting so many of their old haunts was going to be painful enough. Meeting Struan himself could be just that much too traumatic.

43

Again, she decided to leave that to Fate, and got out of the car. The cottage had been let for most of the five years she'd been away, but the tenants had left it only a month ago and it looked as if it was in good order. Slowly, she walked up the flagged path between tall spires of delphiniums and hollyhocks, and unlocked the door.

The cottage welcomed her back as if she had been away only a few days. The tenants had taken good care of it, and had even taken the trouble to replace everything just as they had found it. For a long time Verity could do nothing more than wander about, touching pictures, picking up ornaments and putting them down again, finding herself on a journey of rediscovery. She realised how few things she had taken to London with her, and wondered how she could ever have forgotten so much. The piggy-bank her father had given her on her fifth birthday, the books he had collected—they were all here, smiling at her in a welcome that bore no reproach for her long absence.

At last she went back to the car and carried in her luggage, then set about unpacking the few stores she had brought with her and making a pot of tea. She would have to visit the village shops tomorrow and stock up; the thought of meeting people again was a slightly uneasy one, but she comforted herself that nobody knew the true story, not even Jamie. And she was looking forward to meeting him again. They had kept in touch in a desultory way, with Christmas cards, but she knew little of his life during the past five years. Probably he was married. Anyway, he must be first on her list of visits to make.

As for Struan—he wouldn't figure on the list at all.

Verity was up early next morning, woken by a dawn chorus which sounded as if every bird in the world had gathered outside her window to tell her that a new day had come. She lay for a while, listening and watching the red and gold of a brilliant sunrise, and at last gave up any hope of further sleep and slipped out of bed.

The meadow was silver with dew, the hedges misted with gossamer. Early clouds drifted across the bowl of the sky like wisps of gaudy chiffon, orange, red, and gold, fading eventually to a soft dove grey. Verity leaned from her window, breathing in the cool, fresh air, and wondered how she had ever been able to bear living in London for so long.

Not that it hadn't been a success, she reminded herself. Leaving the secretarial course she had begun locally, she'd been fortunate enough to get a place on one near her sister Sophie's flat, and she'd lived with Sophie until her success as a freelance journalist had enabled her to buy a flat of her own. Now she was a well-known feature writer, her articles on conditions affecting today's woman appearing in all the top glossies, alongside her other speciality, the in-depth interviewing of celebrities from all walks of life. She had even been approached by one of the Sunday colour supplements, but the feature she had written had not yet been published.

So she had achieved the ambition she'd kept secret in her mind all the time she was here. She hadn't even told Struan what she wanted to do, she remembered with a wry twist of her lips. Beside her love for him, all her own ambition had faded away, and it was only when she'd realised finally that her life must be spent without him that she'd thrown herself back into it. That wouldn't happen now, she determined—any love that might come her way in the future would have to accept her as she was, a career woman, with a mind and a life of her own.

But love *had* come her way, hadn't it? And she hadn't

been able to accept it. Wasn't that why she was here—
to lay the old ghosts and go forward, unfettered by the
past?

So wouldn't it be a good idea to stop thinking about
Struan Courtney?

Verity turned away from the window and went to the
tiny bathroom to wash, dressing herself in cool cotton
slacks and shirt. With a cashmere pullover slung round
her shoulders, she stepped out into the garden and
slipped through the meadow gate. Her father had
always loved an early morning walk, she remembered.
And in the quiet that had fallen now that the birds had
stopped their singing, he seemed very close to her.

She was startled, a few minutes later, to see that she
wasn't alone in the meadow. A small child, wearing
jeans and a T-shirt, was already there, kneeling in the
dew-soaked grass and staring intently at a low bank.

'Hullo,' Verity said, coming up behind the child,
'you're up early.'

The small figure jumped violently and whipped
round. It was, Verity could now see, a girl, with dark
hair that curled round her face, grey eyes and small,
delicate features. For a moment they stared at one
another, and Verity noticed the small, square chin that
hinted at a determined, if not stubborn nature, and a
wariness in the large, dark-fringed eyes.

'I'm sorry if I frightened you,' she said mildly. 'I was
just surprised to see someone else here so early. Have
you had your breakfast yet?' She wondered who the
child was. Surely nobody would have sent such a small
girl out alone to play, and it was too early for her to be
going to school yet, or to the shop. In any case, she
looked too young for either.

The child ignored the question. Her first surprise had
gone and she seemed quite cool as she lifted her chin
and said aggrievedly, 'You didn't frighten me. I was

waiting for rabbits to come out. Now you'll have frightened them. I don't expect they'll come now.'

'I'm sorry, I didn't know.' Verity looked at her, feeling helpless. Oughtn't she to find out where the child came from—unless these early-morning excursions were a normal occurrence. 'What's your name?' she asked, 'Mine's Verity.'

'That's a funny name.' The small voice tried to repeat it, without much success. 'I'm Lucy.'

'Lucy? Now, that's a really nice name. Do you live near her, Lucy?'

'Quite near,' Lucy said unforthcomingly. She seemed to think for a minute, then added 'I haven't had my breakfast yet, actually.'

'Well, that's fine—neither have I.' Verity held out her hand. 'Why don't we go and have some together—I live in that cottage—and perhaps the rabbits will venture out while we're away and we can come back and see them.' And perhaps by then I'll have found out who you are, she added silently.

Lucy followed her to the cottage, where they foraged for breakfast and sat down to orange juice and toast. 'I haven't got anything else yet,' Verity explained. 'I only came last night, and I've got to do some shopping. Do you live in the village?'

'No.' Although mollified by the toast and orange juice, Lucy was clearly still suspicious of Verity, or perhaps she was simply annoyed at being interrupted in her wildlife studies. Whatever it was, she seemed willing enough to answer questions while firmly declining to volunteer information. Verity tried again.

'Near the village, then? Or are you on holiday?'

'I don't go to school yet,' Lucy informed her, which Verity took to mean that until you went to school you couldn't be deemed to be on holiday. She also assumed that Lucy must live somewhere nearby. How far would a child of her age walk in search of rabbits? And how far would it be necessary, in an area like this which must be teeming with them? She must live fairly near.

'In one of the houses outside the village?' she persisted, and was rewarded at last. Lucy put down her glass, finished her toast, and—evidently deciding that there was no further point in staying—scrambled down from her stool.

'I live at Courtney Grange,' she announced, making for the door. 'That's my name, too—Lucy Courtney. Now I'll go and see if those rabbits have come out yet.'

Verity sat quite still at the kitchen table, watching the small shabby figure disappear through the door. For a moment she was unable to move. The thoughts whirled through her head, Lucy Courtney—Struan's child. She *had* to be. Struan's and Gina's child. And, from the age she appeared to be, born not too many months after their wedding five years ago.

Was *that* why it had been so hurried? Had Gina been pregnant when Struan had married her? And if so how long had their affair been going on before that?

And why—why couldn't Struan have *told* her? Hadn't he trusted her with the truth? Or was the truth that last, hurtful remark he had flung at her as they finally parted—the fact that he had never loved her at all, only lusted for her?

It took Verity quite a long time to face the fact that she was obliged to return Lucy to her home. It took even longer to persuade Lucy. These early expeditions were, as Verity had suspected, a regular thing, although nobody at Courtney Grange was aware of them. This wasn't, it seemed, from any wish of Lucy's to deceive; simply that she didn't think they'd be interested.

'They're still asleep,' she explained as Verity walked back with her across the meadows. 'And when Daddy gets up he just has his breakfast and goes straight out. He doesn't mind what I do then.'

Doesn't he? Verity thought. Or does he simply never give a thought to his daughter's activities, supposing her to be still in bed? And what about Mummy?

Now that she had actually seen a rabbit—it had been at the entrance to its burrow when Verity had stolen across the grass to fetch her—Lucy seemed to have discarded her uncommunicative attitude, and was ready to chatter about anything and everything as they walked. But most of it passed over Verity's head. Already she was regretting having come. There wasn't really anything else she could have done, she told herself, for there was no telephone at the cottage—but a visit to Courtney Grange on her first morning there was something she definitely hadn't planned. She could only hope that she wouldn't see Struan, that she could simply deliver Lucy to the kitchen door, where she was assured the housekeeper would be up and about, and slip away.

The housekeeper turned out to be Mrs Weedon, who had been at the Grange five years ago, but to Verity's relief she didn't appear to recognise her. She merely shook her head, looking resigned, when Verity and Lucy appeared, and shooed the little girl inside.

'I've told you before, you'll be in trouble if your father finds out about this going out early,' she told Lucy, who gave her an unabashed grin before taking an apple from a basket and slipping through the inner door. 'Now, you'd better go and get washed and changed—you're covered in bits of wet grass. It's good of you to bring her back,' she went on, turning to Verity. 'And to give her breakfast—she doesn't deserve to be spoilt like that.' But her tone was indulgent, and Verity guessed she was fond of Lucy.

'Well, I couldn't find out who she was before she had

breakfast,' Verity answered with a smile. 'And I couldn't let her wander off on her own—you never know who might be about, even early in the morning. Anyway, I won't hold you up, I'm sure you're busy——' She glanced anxiously at the door as she spoke, hoping that Struan wouldn't come to find out who had brought his daughter back. Or Gina . . .

'Oh, Mr Courtney's had his breakfast and gone,' the housekeeper interrupted. 'I was just about to have some coffee—would you like a cup?' A faint frown gathered on her forehead. 'You know, I'm sure I've seen you before. . . .'

Verity gave in. It would be rude to leave without telling Mrs Weedon who she was, and rude not to accept her offer of coffee. And if Struan had gone out. . . . She sat down at the kitchen table, thinking how welcoming and comfortable the big kitchen was, with its pine furnishings and bowls of grasses and wild flowers. 'You have,' she said, smiling. 'I'm Verity Sandison. I used to live at Lane End with my father.'

'Of course!' The bright eyes swept over her, placing the Verity of today with the shy teenager who had been here five years ago. 'You've changed quite a bit. Live in London now, do you?'

'That's right.' Verity wasn't sure whether Mrs Weedon had actually known that, or whether anyone who left the village was automatically assumed to have gone to London. 'But I've come back for a few months—a sort of holiday, and to make up my mind what to do about the cottage. It's been let, as I expect you know, but the tenants have left now and I'm not sure if I want to let it again.'

'Perhaps you'd like to come back to live permanently,' Mrs Weedon suggested, passing her a pottery mug.

'Yes, perhaps.' Verity didn't offer any further comment; she wasn't prepared yet to discuss her nebulous plans with anyone. But she didn't think they would ever include taking up permanent residence at Lane End. She sipped at her coffee, thankful that Struan wasn't likely to appear, but still not too keen to stay and risk seeing Gina. Not that it would matter, since apart from passing in the village once (when Gina's voluptuous good looks had been like a knife in Verity's bruised heart) they'd never met, but ... well, she had never been sure that Struan might not have told Gina all about her. And if he had, and his—wife—found her there... Well, it would be embarrassing, to say the least.

Mrs Weedon seemed glad of her company. She chatted pleasantly while they drank their coffee, telling Verity of various village events that had happened while she was away, and offered her toast which Verity refused. There didn't seem to be any sound from the rest of the house, and Verity wondered if perhaps Gina might be a late riser. All the same, she was anxious to leave as soon as possible, and when the coffee-pot was produced again she shook her head and stood up.

'I really ought to go, thank you very much, Mrs Weedon,' she began. 'I've got quite a lot to——' She was interrupted by the sound of a vehicle in the yard outside. There was the crash of a door, and then a roar.

'Mrs Weedon! Mrs *Weedon*! Damn it, where is the woman?'

'Here, Mr Courtney.' The housekeeper gave Verity a quick glance. 'In the kitchen. We've got a visitor—you'll never guess——' She stopped as Verity, transfixed by the voice which sent shudders vibrating through her body, sent her an imploring glance. A glance which the housekeeper didn't see, for at that moment the doorway was shadowed by the bulk of a man who stood six feet two at least, and was proportionately wide. His voice trailed away as he took in Verity, standing just inside

the door. She looked back at him and felt her heart
jump. And then there was just a long moment of
recognition; recognition that went deeper than the
normal remembering of face and feature.

'My God,' Struan Courtney said slowly. 'It's Verity.'

By the time Struan had recovered from his surprise and
had organised Mrs Weedon to bring them more coffee,
this time in the drawing-room, Verity had begun to
regret ever having brought Lucy home. It wasn't what
she'd intended at all; she'd meant simply to see the child
safely back and then slip away. Seeing Struan hadn't
been any part of her plan. Hadn't she made up her
mind to leave that to Fate? But Fate had played a cruel
trick on her, and had lost no time in doing so. Finding
her here, Struan could think nothing else but that she'd
been unable to wait to see him, had grabbed at the first
chance. He'd think she'd been yearning for him all these
years. And whether that was the truth or not, she
wasn't going to have him believing it. He'd hurt her far
too much five years ago to be given a chance to do it
again.

Besides which, he was married, and his wife was
presumably somewhere in the house. What was *she*
going to think if she found them together? Or didn't
Struan care about that?

'Little Verity,' Struan said wonderingly when Mrs
Weedon had gone. He crossed to the window and
turned to look at her, his eyes wary. Since that first
moment of recognition he seemed to have dropped a
shutter across his face, leaving it carefully blank, ready
for whatever expression he chose to allow. 'Well, who'd
have thought it? You've grown up.'

Verity felt a spasm of irritation. She felt sure that
Struan was deliberately hiding his real self from her,
shutting her out. He was patronising her in order to

make her feel once again the gauche teenager he remembered. Perhaps it was a kind of defence—perhaps he was the one who felt insecure now, meeting her again as a confident, attractive woman. It wasn't surprising really, she supposed. Their last meeting had been electric with barely-suppressed emotion.

'Grown up? Well, we're all five years older,' she said crisply. 'I daresay quite a lot has happened to us both in that time. Not that I've time to discuss it now, unfortunately, and I'll have to forgo the coffee. I've a million things to do at the cottage.' She began to get up from the chair he'd shown her to, but his quick movement had her sitting down again. He was *not* going to touch her! She leaned back, fighting for self-possession, looking up at him.

'Nothing that won't wait, I'm sure,' he said pleasantly, and she shivered. Surely he didn't mean to keep her here by force!

Quickly, searching for some safe topic of conversation, she said, 'You've a nice little girl.'

'That's right. Lucy.' A shadow crossed his face, 'A considerable responsibility, children.'

'It's something most of us take on, though.' Play it cool, Verity told herself. He can't keep you here for ever. He must have work to do, and surely Gina will put in an appearance ... She found she was almost looking forward to meeting Struan's wife. Anything which would ease the tension that came from being alone with Struan.

Struan turned his head sharply. 'You've children?' he asked, and there was an urgency in his voice which shook her. What could it matter to him if she had children? He'd discarded her long ago, hadn't he? Maybe he'd had a conscience after all—a conscience that still troubled him over the way he'd treated her. Maybe he needed to know that she was happy.

Well, she couldn't give him that satisfaction, but neither did she intend to give him any idea of how he still affected her. And he did—to herself, she had to admit it. The pulsating attraction was still there ... She closed her eyes momentarily, telling herself that he mustn't guess, filled with a mixture of wild exhilaration that what she felt for Struan was real love and not infatuation, and a deep, grinding despair because it could never be any good. Struan didn't love her—he was merely a part of that mutual attraction, which for him went no further than that. And more than that, he was married to Gina; he was, as Ann had prophesied, a family man—although he didn't have the paunch and he certainly wasn't dull—and he was as far as ever out of her reach. Probably farther.

She opened her eyes and forced herself to look coolly at Struan. His eyes were still that same light, silvery grey, she noticed. But there had been other changes; small ones, but all adding up to something that disturbed her. Those tiny lines around his eyes, surely they hadn't been there before? And had his mouth had quite that bitter twist when he spoke? The hair waving away from his forehead was as thick, but wasn't that a dusting of silver there too? He's aged, she thought with a sudden pang, and aged more than a man should in five years. He's only thirty-five—what's happened to carve those lines, to give him that haunted expression?

She wondered again where Gina was.

Struan got up abruptly, uncoiling his long body from the chair in one lithe movement and striding over to the window. He hadn't lost any of that vibrant energy, she noticed, though he held himself tensely, as though afraid to let it loose. There was a tautness in his muscles, a hint of suppressed vitality that reminded her of a tiger she had once seen in a zoo, pacing restlessly and endlessly about its cage. The frustrated power of the animal had reached out to her, and in that moment she had shared in its despair. But surely Struan couldn't be in despair?

He spoke without looking at her, still staring out of the window.

'Tell me why you really came here.'

'If you mean why did I come to Courtney Grange, it was simply to make sure that Lucy got home safely,' she replied promptly. 'Otherwise, I decided on having a few months' holiday, between jobs.' It wasn't the moment now to tell him of her career, of the in-depth interviews, of the biography she hoped to write. 'And as the the cottage was empty, it seemed a good opportunity to come and sort things out.' She watched him with a curiosity that was rapidly developing into real anxiety. There was something here that she didn't understand—something that was burning Struan up, gnawing at his strength. It couldn't be any help to him to be reminded of the raw emotion that had torn at them just before his wedding. Maybe she shouldn't have come after all, she thought ruefully, maybe she should have gone abroad, perhaps to stay with Sophie in New York. But it was too late for that now; she'd committed herself. And in any case, she had to *know*. . . .

'You really expect me to believe that?' he demanded roughly, swinging round to face her. His expression was shadowed now, but his whole body was taut, expressing an electric tension in every line. 'You've changed, Verity. You were an innocent, untouched girl when I knew you before. You were wide-eyed and bewildered and you reached to my heart. Now——' he made a gesture '—now, you're a woman, you've matured, you look at me with the eyes of experience. Whatever you've done since we knew each other five years ago, it's given you a poise you never dreamed of then. You've clearly done well for yourself, whatever jobs you've had in the

meantime have been well-paid, your clothes tell me
that, and that expensive gold watch on your wrist. In
fact, you have all the signs of being a successful,
confident, liberated businesswoman.'

He paused, watching her, while Verity struggled to
keep her own expression impassive. He'd come
altogether too near the truth there, seen too much. How
could she have hoped to deceive him, when he knew her
so well, when he'd always known her so well? 'So why
come back to Lane End?' he went on, almost as if
speaking to himself. 'Why come back to a dead-end
village at the back of nowhere to bury yourself? Why
aren't you in London, where you obviously belong,
living the kind of life you've evidently become
accustomed to? Why bury yourself in the country?'

'Perhaps I don't want that kind of life any more,'
Verity said evenly. 'I've always liked the country. And
anyway, that's my business, isn't it? I just felt like a
change.'

Struan moved away from the window and she was
shocked to see the lines deepen on his face, as if he were
in some kind of pain. He turned to her again, leaning
this time on the mantelpiece. He looked completely at
home in the big, graceful drawing-room. Behind him
there was a photograph—a wedding-group which
Verity suddenly realised must be his. Again she
wondered about Gina. Where was she? And what had
happened between her and Struan to bring those bitter
lines to his face?

'Let me go now, Struan,' she said quietly. 'You must
see that there's nothing for us to talk about.'

He had been staring into the fireplace as if lost in
thought, perhaps in memories, but now he looked up.
His silver eyes speared into hers, and Verity felt the
familiar jerk of her heart, the spiral of desire in her
stomach. Oh, Struan, she thought yearningly, why

couldn't it work out for us? Why couldn't you have loved me as I loved you—as I still love you, deeply though you hurt me? It was a mistake to have come, she told herself unhappily. She'd stirred up old memories and found them just as potent, just as painful. She ought to have stayed away; accepted that she would never love anyone else; made the best of a life without love.

'Nothing?' he repeated, and his voice was rough. 'Yes, maybe you're right, Verity—there's nothing for us to say any more. Or maybe there's just one thing—one thing that may give you some satisfaction, one thing you may not know but will soon find out.' He paused and stared down at her, his eyes dark with a pain which was deeper than any she had yet seen, and which shocked her. 'My marriage to Gina didn't work out, you see. It was over a year ago. Our divorce was made final in May.' His face twisted with a bitterness that wrenched at her heart. 'So let me ask you again, Verity,' he said raggedly. 'Just why are you here? Why did you come? What in heaven's name did you think I might have to offer you now?'

CHAPTER FOUR

VERITY sat quite still. Struan's words echoed round the room, their harshness an ugly anomaly among the comfort of the furnishings. Someone—Gina?—had put a lot of thought into this room, Verity thought, vaguely noting the floral patterns of the big, squashy chairs and sofas, the quality of the huge Persian carpet, the elegant watered silk that covered the walls. It was a room for relaxing, for forgetting the troubles of the outside world, not a room for quarrelling and harsh words. But if the troubles were inside, rather than out . . .?

She realised that Struan was staring at her, waiting for an answer to his bitter questions. But what answer could she give him? How could she tell him that what had happened between them before his marriage had dogged her for the past five years, that she had come back to Lane End in an effort to pick up the threads of her life before it had begun to go so terribly wrong? What could that mean to him, when he so obviously had his own anguished memories to torture him? Memories that had nothing to do with her, memories she could barely guess at.

She made a helpless gesture with one hand.

'Struan, I'm sorry, I didn't know. . . . I hadn't heard about you and Gina, I swear it. And I didn't come to seek you out—I came because I wanted time to—to take stock. And to decide what to do about the cottage.'

'How long have you been back?' he asked in a flat tone, and Verity sighed.

'I arrived last night.' She saw his nod, and added

58

angrily: 'And I *didn't* take the first opportunity I had of coming up here in the hope of seeing you! My God, Struan, what do you think I am?' She was on her feet now, facing him, a furious rage sweeping through her. 'I tell you, I didn't know anything about your divorce—and if I had, do you think I would have come hotfoot back here to beg you to take me up where you left me five years ago? Do you think I've no more pride than that—and after what you did to me?' She let her eyes rake him with all the scorn she could muster, and added contemptuously, 'Do you really think that in all those years I haven't had more than enough opportunity to wipe out your memory? Do you imagine that what I felt for you was any more than a particularly immature puppy-love?'

She saw Struan's colour recede, leaving his face ashen, and swung away. Her breath was coming rapidly, her heart thumping, and she could feel the heat of anger in her cheeks. She stood quite still for a moment, fighting to regain her control, knowing that she needed every ounce of it. Where Struan was concerned, her emotions were all too near the surface. And although he had hurt her profoundly, she knew that the magnetism he had for her was still as powerful as ever, that with a word, a touch, even a look, he could have her as weak and helpless as she had been at eighteen.

She heard him move behind her, and tensed. But he made no attempt to touch her, and when he spoke his voice was dry and quiet, as if his throat ached.

'I'm sorry, Verity. You're quite right, of course. What happened between us was years ago and nothing to do with the people we are today. And since you're back, it would be foolish for us to be anything other than friends.' She turned slowly, unbelievingly. He was standing quite still, one hand held out towards her, but she got the impression that what he was saying wasn't easy for him. 'Let's be friends, Verity,' he said, and this time she was sure she heard a note of sincerity in his voice.

'Of course we can be friends,' she said stiffly, but she dared not take his hand, and after a moment he let it fall back at his side. 'And—and I would like some coffee, please.' She would be awash with the stuff if she drank much more, but at least once they'd been through the ritual she would be free to go. She watched as Struan poured it out, and accepted her cup with a nod of thanks.

'Lucy seems a happy little thing,' she remarked after a moment.

'Yes, she's quite well-balanced. I'm looking for a nanny for her at present—not had much success, though I've got an applicant coming later this morning. That's why I came back. I'd forgotten to tell Mrs Weedon to expect her.' He spoke in a clipped, formal voice, stirring his coffee without looking at her, and Verity bit her lip. This was being every bit as difficult as she had envisaged. How *could* they be friends?

'I imagine she's a fairly easy child,' she said lamely, and Struan shrugged.

'If she wants to be.'

Oh God, she thought, this is awful. They were actually making polite conversation! Yet she could have sworn that there was still some powerful emotion raging inside him, though just what it was she couldn't be sure. Perhaps he really had loved Gina, hadn't wanted the divorce. Or was it to do with Verity's own arrival? She remembered his words as he'd told her to leave him, just before his wedding. Was he still affected by her, still tormented by a frustrated desire that he was ashamed of because it had nothing to do with love? Or had the whole impression been her own imagination, the result of projecting her own feelings on to him—wishful thinking, in other words? Perhaps he was merely embarrassed by her appearance, by the memory of his own behaviour just before his wedding.

'I'll have to go soon,' she said at last, desperate to break down the barrier that seemed to have risen between them. 'Could I just say goodbye to Lucy?'

He hesitated, then shrugged. Perhaps he saw the advantage of using Lucy as a buffer between them. 'Yes, all right. She'll be with Mrs Weedon in the kitchen. I'll go and fetch her.' He got up and strode from the room, leaving Verity to slump momentarily in her chair. The tension between them was as taut as wire, and already she felt exhausted. It *couldn't* just be imagination. There was something there—a deep, strictly controlled dynamo of feeling, to which she responded as automatically as if he had pressed a switch.

It didn't have to be something that concerned her, though. In fact, it was really rather unlikely, after all these years. It was far more likely to be Gina and the divorce.

Whatever it was, Verity knew that it was going to be very difficult to go away from Courtneys this morning, knowing that this time it must be for ever. The past half-hour had shown her quite clearly where her own feelings lay, and the uselessness of them. And she was going to have to make her way through the rest of her life bearing that knowledge. Alone. The thought left her feeling chilled and oddly bereft.

At the sound of returning footsteps, she sat up again, determined not to let Struan guess at what she was feeling. That would only make things worse. She lifted a bright smile on to her face and turned expectantly towards the door.

The sight of Lucy with her father gave Verity another

shock, and she wondered why she hadn't seen the truth immediately. Thin, dark, with light grey eyes that could be disconcertingly cool, and a chin that was nothing short of stubborn—there was no mistaking whose child this was. Lucy Courtney could have been a miniature of her father, and it was only because Verity hadn't expected it that she hadn't seen the resemblance at once.

'Hullo, Lucy,' she said. 'I've got to go now. I just wanted to say goodbye.'

'Oh, do you really have to go?' Lucy asked in a tone that showed she wasn't just copying grown-up manners. 'I wanted to show you Mr Macgregor. Does she have to go, Daddy?' she appealed, turning her face up to her father.

'If she says so, yes.' He had got back his own control while he was out of the room, Verity saw, and his mouth was grim. 'And you aren't to go bothering Miss Sandison over at Lane End either, Lucy, do you understand? Especially at six o'clock in the morning.'

Lucy looked mutinous, but before she could say any more Mrs Weedon looked in, her expression apologetic.

'I'm sorry, Mr Courtney, but Matthews is at the door, he wants a word if it's not inconvenient. Something to do with the sheep on Low Pasture.'

Struan sighed. 'All right, I'll come right away.' He glanced at Verity. 'I'll have to ask you to see yourself out, I'm afraid. Help yourself to more coffee if you want it. Lucy, you'd better go back with Mrs Weedon——'

'Oh, no,' Lucy protested. 'I can stay with Verry, can't I? She said I could call her Verry. And I could show her Mr Macgregor. She's *interested*—aren't you, Verry? You will stay for a while, won't you?'

'If you want me to,' Verity said cautiously, and caught an odd look from Struan that she couldn't quite interpret. Was he pleased or not? She couldn't tell, but at the moment she was more concerned with Lucy. She hadn't missed the way the little girl's hand had clung to her father's, or the sudden desperate loneliness that had revealed itself in the babyish face. 'I'd like to meet Mr Macgregor,' she added, wondering who he was. The gardener, perhaps?

'Oh, all right, then. Be it on your own head,' Struan added to Verity. 'And don't let her keep you too long from those million things you have to do back at the cottage.' He gave her a flick of a smile as he spoke that caught at her heart. It was almost the smile he had given her before—tender and teasing, the smile that said *I love you.* But almost before she had realised it, it was gone and he was speaking to Lucy again. 'Behave yourself, now. I won't be long. Tell Miss Sandison about your rabbits.' He gave Verity a wry look. 'There were thirteen at the last count.'

'Good heavens,' Verity said as he closed the door, 'are you breeding them?'

'No, they're doing it themselves,' Lucy answered seriously. 'Can I have a biscuit, please?' She chose one from the plate, then sat down on the floor. 'I'm going to be a rabbit-farmer,' she added through a mouthful of crumbs.

'Well, you seem to have made a good start. Thirteen rabbits is quite a flock. Or should it be herd? What are you going to do with them?'

'I don't know.' Lucy chewed her biscuit thoughtfully. 'Daddy says I ought to sell them. But I wouldn't want them to be eaten.'

'Perhaps people would buy them for pets. What does Mummy say?'

'Mummy? Oh, Mummy hasn't seen them. She doesn't like animals much, anyway. Can I have some milk, please?'

Verity poured milk into a cup. She wondered why Lucy was living at Courtney Grange instead of with Gina. But she couldn't question Lucy about her mother.

'Would you like to see my rabbits?' Lucy enquired, and Verity nodded.

'Yes, I would. Let's go as soon as you've finished your milk, shall we?' There was no knowing how long Struan would be, and the opportunity to spend some time with this miniature edition of him was too good to resist. Lucy had a gravity that charmed her, though Verity was still worried by that slightly elusive quality which she had noticed in the cool, silvery eyes. It was as if Lucy were only half-child, half-pixie, and might vanish if you tried to hold her too firmly.

She followed Lucy through the hall and down a narrow corridor to a side door. This led out to a small garden, enclosed by a low lonicera hedge, and evidently Lucy's own domain. A swing stood in one corner with a doll leaning drunkenly against one of the ropes. A wheelbarrow, a trowel and a heap of tumbled earth were evidence of gardening activities, while close by someone had dug a deeper hole which was lined with blue plastic and apparently destined to become a pond. At one side of the garden there was a shed, and it was here that Lucy led Verity to inspect the rabbits.

'That's Mr Macgregor,' Lucy began, indicating a large black rabbit lying somnolent in one corner of the big hutch. 'He and Mrs Macgregor are the mother and father. They've got six children now. They're with Mrs Macgregor because she's got their milk. The ones in that hutch are the first family they had.' She regarded the small, furry bodies. 'They're nice, aren't they? Daddy says we'll have a lot more soon if we keep them all together.'

'I'm sure you will.' Verity was reminded of an old

song she'd heard about a boy who had had two rabbits and ended up with more than he could count. *And look what's coming through the door—MORE!* 'Does Daddy think that's a good idea?' she enquired cautiously.

Whether Daddy thought it a good idea or not didn't seem to be very important to Lucy, and Verity guessed that there were battles ahead. Lucy was clearly fascinated by the endless capabilities of rabbits to produce more rabbits. 'And all out of lettuce leaves and stuff,' she informed Verity in a tone of wonder. Verity allowed herself to speculate on the views of the new nanny regarding rabbits. It could make all the difference in Lucy's acceptance of her.

They spent some time discussing the rabbits, going on to the planning of Lucy's garden—her main idea being to plant groundsel, dandelions and chickweed as feed for them. Verity couldn't quite bring herself to tell Lucy that these plants would probably grow anyway, and reflected that the spectacular success which Lucy's garden was bound to enjoy could only encourage her. By the time she went on to more conventional crops, she would be hooked.

It was almost half an hour before she saw Struan coming out of the kitchen door, his face grim. Verity watched him for a moment, her heart aching. She knew that when she left the cottage this time, she would be leaving Struan for ever. She almost wished she had never come—but knew that she'd had no real choice. She'd had to see him again, if only to sort out her own tangled emotions. The fact that she now knew quite clearly that she had not outgrown her love for him didn't make things any easier; but at least she knew why she'd never been able to love anyone else.

'I'm sorry,' Struan said abruptly, coming to stand beside her. 'I didn't intend that you should be left so long with Lucy. She ought to have gone back to Mrs

Weedon.' He gave his daughter an admonishing glance.
'I hope you haven't been a nuisance.'

'No, I haven't.' The little girl's voice was indignant,
and Verity noticed with amusement how like her father
she was, standing with lifted chin to glower up at him.
'Verry was *interested*.' She hadn't managed to get her
tongue round 'Verity' yet. 'She *likes* rabbits. And
gardening.'

Struan gave Verity a wry glance. 'In fact, you're not
far short of perfect,' he murmured. 'Exactly what I'd
hoped for from Miss Morris—the new nanny.'

Something in his tone caught at Verity's attention.
'*Had* hoped for? Isn't she coming after all?'

'God knows,' Struan said frustratedly. 'I've just had a
message to say she's been in a car accident. Broken leg
and cracked ribs, apparently. Nothing more serious, as
far as they can tell at present, but obviously she won't
be fit for a couple of months at least.' He sighed, his
mouth settling into hard lines. 'It looks as if we'll have
to find someone else to fill in—just what I didn't want.
Oh, Mrs Weedon's been very good, but she can't cope
with a live-wire like young Lucy, not as well as her
other work, and it's not fair to expect it of her.' He ran
a hand through his hair, and Verity longed to touch
him, to slide her own fingers through the loose black
waves. 'But what Lucy needs is continuity. A succession
of temporary nannies is the last thing . . .' He sighed.

What about Gina? Verity wondered yet again. What
was stopping her from looking after her own child?
Even if Struan had been awarded custody—was she
such a bad mother that he couldn't ask her to take care
of Lucy in an emergency? Or did Gina herself refuse the
responsibility? But there was no time to think about
that now. Struan was glancing at his watch, an obvious
hint that it was time she went, and she was beginning to
feel herself that to stay much longer in his company,

having to repress her feelings, was going to be more painful than she could bear. She had told him that the memory of what had happened between them had been wiped out long ago. If only that were true!

But she couldn't afford to let Struan know the truth.

'Well, you can always let Lucy come over to Lane End for a few hours,' she said lightly. 'I've had quite a lot of experience with children, as it happens—I did a couple of summers as an au pair while I was at school, and again when I was at college after Dad died. I'd be quite glad of her company. Anyway——' she glanced at her own watch '—I'll have to be going now. Thank you for the coffee. And for showing me the Macgregors,' she said to Lucy. 'And if you want to come and watch the rabbits in the field, come at any time—only let Daddy or Mrs Weedon know first, all right?'

'All right,' Lucy said reluctantly. 'But if they're asleep when I go——'

'We won't be, because there'll be no more early-morning walks,' Struan interrupted firmly. 'At least, not on your own. I'll take you out myself sometimes if you like—but not *every* morning. I have to be up and about quite early enough to work.'

With that, Lucy had to be satisfied. She shook hands gravely with Verity and invited her to come and visit the Macgregors as often as she liked. Verity smiled down into the solemn grey eyes, so like Struan's, and felt a pang. If things had been different, this could be her daughter, hers and Struan's. But it hadn't worked out like that. Her dreams had been shattered, and at a time when she was least fitted to cope. And the hurt had been gnawing at her ever since.

During the next week or two, Lucy became a regular visitor to Lane End, although Verity saw nothing of Struan. It became an accepted routine that Lucy would

come over the meadow immediately after lunch, leaving
Mrs Weedon to have a quiet afternoon by herself. The
housekeeper was clearly fond of Lucy but found her
exhausting—which Verity could well understand.

'I wish *you* could be my nanny,' Lucy remarked one
afternoon as they came back from a ramble through the
woods. 'Why can't you? You could come and live with
us then. It would be better than that tiny cottage.'

'I like Lane End,' Verity protested, but she was
smiling although her heart had missed a beat at the
thought of living at Courtney Grange with Lucy—and
Struan. 'Can't Daddy find a new nanny for you, then?'

Lucy shrugged. 'Some have come to see him but we
didn't like any of them.' She paused, then added
indignantly, 'There was one Daddy thought would be
all right, but she didn't like the Macgregors. And she
had a dog. A terrier.'

'Who presumably did,' Verity added. 'No, that
wouldn't have done.'

'I don't really see why I need a nanny, anyway,' Lucy
said thoughtfully. 'Mrs Weedon doesn't mind if I'm
only home in the mornings, and I can come and see you
in the afternoons, and Daddy usually puts me to bed.
And I'll be going to school in September.'

Verity felt a stab of pity for the little girl. She could
understand Struan's anxiety—Lucy needed someone
who would be looking after her exclusively, not just as
an added responsibility. Someone who would have her
interests at heart—who would love her. A mother . . .
But since she apparently couldn't have that, a nanny
had to be the next best thing.

'But I shan't be here for ever,' she pointed out. 'And
Mrs Weedon's got a lot to do around the house.' She was
older too, she thought, old enough to be Lucy's
grandmother. Fine for the odd few hours—but every day
. . .? And what about when Struan needed to be away?

'I wish you could be my nanny,' Lucy said again, and broke into a short run that took her several yards ahead. 'Can we have iced lemonade when we get back to the cottage?'

It shouldn't, Verity supposed, have come as a surprise when she saw Struan at the cottage gate a few evenings later, his lean face serious. Her heart thudding, she opened the door and watched him come up the path. In spite of his suggestion that they should be friends, she didn't imagine for a moment that this could be a casual social call. Struan wouldn't have come to Lane End without a purpose.

Was he going to tell her not to see any more of Lucy?

'Hullo, Struan,' she said, keeping her voice light. 'You've come just in time, I was about to make coffee. Or would you prefer something stronger.'

'Coffee will be fine.' He followed her inside, stooping through the low doorway. 'I hope I'm not interrupting anything important.'

'Of course you're not.' Polite conversation again, she thought ruefully. We might be strangers, instead of—— She jerked her mind sharply away and went into the tiny kitchen to put the kettle on, her fingers trembling as she held it under the tap. Struan was altogether too big for this cottage—his presence seemed to fill every corner. 'We'll have it in the garden, shall we?' she continued brightly. 'It's too nice to stay indoors.'

Struan stood looking at her. He seemed to fill the doorway and Verity was uneasily aware that, if he cared to, he could trap her in the confined space of the kitchen. She threw an involuntary glance at the window and felt her colour deepen as she saw his eyes follow hers. She had the uncomfortable thought that he knew exactly what was in her mind.

Thankfully, she saw that the kettle was boiling and spooned coffee into the two mugs, setting them on a tray with a plate of shortbread. 'It's only instant, I'm afraid,' she said, her back to him as she poured the water. 'I get into bad habits when I'm on my own.'

'Instant's quite all right.' He stood back to let her pass him, but even so she couldn't help brushing against his body and the contact sent a shiver through her. The tray shook in her hands and she heard the faint rattle of spoons. Praying that Struan hadn't heard it too, she went past him and out into the garden.

There was a low wooden table in front of the garden seat which she and her father had put at the edge of the tiny lawn, and she set the tray down on it. It was a pity there weren't two seats, so that they could avoid any further contact, but to go in and fetch a chair would be too obvious. To her relief, Struan seemed to want contact as little as she did. He sat down beside her, his arm carefully not touching hers, and she was reminded of that other time when he had taken care to keep himself slightly apart from her. But that was when they'd only just met for the first time, and had both been equally shaken by the desire that had flared so unexpectedly between them.

It was different now. Something had happened to kill Struan's love for her—if it had ever been real—and made him turn to Gina. And now that had gone wrong too.

Through her own remembered pain, Verity could still feel compassion for whatever it was he had been through. Her own bewildered unhappiness could still be shot through with tenderness.

But that's because I love him still, she thought, looking for a moment at the dark head, dusted now with a few strands of early grey. And that's something I have to learn to live with.

'I hope Lucy's not being a nuisance to you,' Struan

said, breaking the silence. 'She comes over most days, I believe. If you'd rather she didn't——'

'Oh no, I like to see her,' Verity assured him, and it was true. During the past week or so she had become very fond of the odd, serious little girl with her pixie face and the grey eyes that were so like Struan's. She was sorry for her too, aware of the fact that the child must be missing her mother, although she seemed quite matter-of-fact about the situation. All the same, a five-year-old *needed* a mother. Being shuttled about between her father, a housekeeper and a stranger who wasn't even going to be around for very long just wasn't enough ... 'You can let her come whenever she likes,' she added, hoping that Struan wasn't going to stop Lucy's visits. 'I meant what I said. I'm having a rest, and there's nothing special I'd be doing anyway. Lucy's good company.'

'Hardly restful, I'd have thought.' Struan turned his head suddenly, and she felt a slight shock as she met his eyes. What was it that haunted them, that filled them with such dark, unfathomable trouble? 'Verity, there was something I wanted to ask you—it's difficult . . .'

Verity waited, her breath stilled. Surely he wasn't going to tell her that he'd made a mistake—that after all this time it was she—No! It couldn't be as simple as that, and she wasn't even sure she wanted it to be. She loved him, yes; that was ingrained in every last, tiny fibre of her. But trust him? That was something quite different.

'You'll probably think I'm crazy even to consider it,' he said at last. 'I suppose I wouldn't, if I weren't desperate. But well, you know what my situation is. Damned awkward, to say the least. It doesn't look as if Miss Morris is going to be fit for at least a couple of months, and I haven't been able to find anyone else suitable.' Slowly, it dawned on Verity that he was still talking about his problems with Lucy. 'I just wondered—Lucy seems to have taken to you, and since you say you like having her around and don't seem to have anything else special to do—well, would *you* consider taking over? Just until Miss Morris can come.' His eyes met hers again, oddly diffident yet pleading. 'It's a lot to ask, I know. You can't really want a job as a nanny, especially when you'd intended having a holiday. But since you see a lot of her anyway—well, what do you think?'

Verity stared at him. She had never known Struan so ill at ease, so uncertain of himself. Although with perfect justification, when you considered what he was doing—asking her, the girl who'd hoped to marry him, to look after the daughter of the woman he'd virtually jilted her for! It was almost funny, she thought ironically, except that she felt more like crying. Well, she could take comfort from one thing—Struan clearly had no inkling that her feelings for him hadn't changed, no idea that they were in fact stronger than ever. Her efforts to hide them from him had obviously been spectacularly successful.

'I'm sorry,' Struan said when she didn't speak. 'I shouldn't have asked you. I quite understand—I won't bother you again——' He began to get up.

'No!' Almost without thinking, Verity put out her hand and caught at his arm. The shock of contact was still there, but she knew that it must be only on her side. The magnetic attraction that had been between them was now only one-way. Struan had proved that five years ago, and proved it again now by coming here tonight. 'No, please don't go yet—you haven't drunk your coffee. And you haven't given me time to think it over. This—this idea has come as something of a surprise, you know.'

'Yes, of course it has.' He sat back again, but he

wasn't relaxed, she could feel his tension quivering in the air between them. 'Well, just say no and we'll forget it. I oughtn't to have asked you. It was a crazy idea— only I'm rather desperate, you see. Mrs Weedon's due to go away on holiday soon, and I don't want to ask her to cancel it—she's already done quite enough. And, as I said, I just don't seem able to find anyone suitable.'

Verity took a deep breath. She hadn't thought it over at all, hadn't given herself time to consider the implications. But there were times when consideration wasn't a good idea. Like when you were about to dive from a high board into cold water. Or into a blazing tank of fire, as she'd once seen a man do at a fairground.

But presumably he'd known he was safe. And the diver would know that he could swim. Whereas she . . .

'I'll do it,' she heard herself saying. 'I'll be happy to help out. When would you like me to start?'

She went over to Courtney Grange next morning. It felt odd to be driving there instead of walking across the meadow—she couldn't remember ever having done such a thing before. She swung the car through the tall wrought-iron gates and up the long, curving drive. The house was there, proud on its grassy knoll; as she came nearer she could see the long terrace that ran along the front, with wide steps leading up to the door. The two daily cleaners were there already, one cleaning windows, the other polishing the brass door-knocker, and the old gardener was tidying up some flowerbeds. Verity stopped the car and felt panic grip her. For a brief, searing moment, she wished she hadn't come.

Looking after Lucy on an 'official' basis wouldn't be any kind of a problem, except that it would mean spending time here instead of at the cottage. What had shaken her was the realisation that Struan expected her to live in.

'Live in!' she'd echoed as they sat in her small garden, watching the gathering dusk. 'But surely that's not necessary—you only need me during the day, and in any case Lucy and I can spend a good deal of our time here——'

'That won't be suitable,' he interrupted sharply. 'I want Lucy to grow up in her own home, not someone else's. Oh, I know this is only temporary—but it's continuity she needs. A proper routine in her own home. That's the only way I can give her any kind of security, don't you understand that?'

Verity had understood that, and had shrugged her shoulders in agreement. But living at Courtney Grange, in daily contact with Struan, had been no part of her plan when she had come back. Seeing him occasionally was bad enough. She wasn't at all sure she could cope with more.

But that was something she couldn't tell him. This was no time to acknowledge her real feelings, much less let Struan guess at them. So far, she had given no hint that her return to Lane End was anything more than a sabbatical, a few months' rest while she decided what to do with the cottage. If she could only keep things on that level—make Struan believe that what had happened between them was no more than an adolescent memory—she might have a chance.

A chance of what? Of keeping her self-respect—nothing more than that. And, perhaps, of achieving what she had come here to do: marking the file on Struan, that file in her heart which said 'unfinished business', with a firm CLOSED. So that she could go back to London and get on with her life.

Perhaps, after all, living at Courtney Grange might be a good idea. Not seeing Straun for five years hadn't cut him out of her heart. Seeing him every day might—just—work the miracle.

'All right,' she said, 'I'll move in. Provided you don't mind my bringing Lucy here sometimes. There are things I need to do, and she wouldn't be neglected. In fact, she seems to enjoy helping.'

'I don't mind at all,' Struan said. 'So long as you're living at the Grange; so long as it's the place you come back to.'

Verity turned her head sharply, but he wasn't looking at her. His eyes were on the ancient, gnarled apple tree in the far corner of the crowded garden. She could only see his cool, impassive profile, and there was nothing to tell her whether she had imagined that odd note in his voice; the note that had seemed to indicate some deeper meaning to his words.

With an impatient shrug, Verity got out of her car and went up the steps into the house. She was barely inside the door when Lucy erupted from the kitchen and launched herself into Verity's arms. Verity caught her, laughing and staggering, and became aware of Struan, close behind, watching them with unreadable eyes.

She looked down quickly at the child, seeing with pleasure that the wariness had completely vanished from Lucy's grey eyes now, to be replaced by a shining excitement. The soft fingers tightened round hers.

'You're staying with me!' Lucy exclaimed, jigging up and down. 'Isn't it lovely? I asked Daddy and asked him, and in the end he said yes.' She turned to her father. 'I like Verry. She likes my rabbits. I'll do what she tells me *all* the time.'

Struan and Verity exchanged glances. The tension was still there, she realised, but it was muted this morning, and she grinned as his mouth twitched with amusement.

'Love me, love my rabbits,' he murmured. 'Well, let's hope it lasts. I seem to be under petticoat rule here.

Now, if you don't mind, I've got to see my farm manager.' He looked down at Lucy, who was remaining quiet with obvious difficulty. 'Now, don't forget, Verity isn't really a nanny, and she's being very kind to come here and look after you during her holiday. So I'm relying on you for good behaviour, you understand? No tricks, and no arguing.'

'No, Daddy,' Lucy said with a meekness that made him look at her sharply. He hesitated, as if he wanted to say more, then shrugged, gave Verity another glance which was a mixture of relief, bafflement and—wasn't that some other emotion? Verity couldn't quite analyse it. Then he turned and strode quickly from the house.

Verity found she'd been holding her breath. She let it out on a sigh.

'You're staying!' Lucy abandoned her docility and began to leap about, chanting at the top of her voice, 'Verry's staying! Verry's staying! Hooray, horray, Verry can stay!' She stopped breathless, eyes sparkling, grinning from ear to ear and looking more like a pixie than ever as she demanded, 'Did you hear me make up a poem then? Did you hear it? Isn't it *lovely*, Verry— isn't it?'

'Yes,' Verity said, smiling down at the excited child. She held out her hands and clasped Lucy's, dancing with her in a circle as if she too were only five years old. What on earth have you got yourself into now? she wondered ruefully. Acting as a nanny to the child of a man who jilted you five years ago—it's crazy. And it can't do any good. It can only lead to trouble.

'Yes,' she said again, and caught Lucy to her and hugged her. 'Yes, it's *lovely*.'

CHAPTER FIVE

FOR the first few days she spent at Courtney Grange, except for the first evening, when Lucy had gone to bed and she and Struan sat down to discuss the situation, Verity saw little of him. His presence filled the house— but his absence tore at her heart.

'I've decided to visit Miss Morris some time next week, when she's recovered a little from the accident,' he told Verity when she came down from seeing Lucy into bed. 'She'll have some idea then of how long she'll be on the sick list, and I'll know whether I want to go ahead with her appointment. It's all very indeterminate where you're concerned, I'm afraid. I simply don't know how long it's going to be. It's completely disrupting your holiday—and what about your own job? Have you got extended leave? I can't be responsible for your own career being interrupted.'

I ought to tell him the truth, Verity thought uneasily. But if she did, what then? Struan wasn't likely to accept any offer to stay once he knew that she was really a successful freelance journalist, writing in most of the glossy magazines. She could remember his antagonism towards journalists, brought about mainly by his brother Justin's appearance in so many gossip columns. Clearly, he didn't know that she had gone into that world herself—he probably thought she was simply a secretary, albeit a rather high-powered one. 'It's all right,' she heard herself say. 'I'm between jobs at the moment and not really worried about another just yet. I've enough saved to be able to look around for just the right thing, and I might as well be here as anywhere while I do it.' Had she overdone the casualness, she wondered, adding, 'And since I like Lucy and she seems to have taken to me. . . .'

'All right, then.' Struan seemed about to add something, but apparently decided against it. Verity watched him, torn with a desire to go over to him, sit close, nestle against that strong body. The last five years seemed to have faded, as if they were a dream. Was it really so long since those summer days when they'd walked in the meadows and kissed? Had there really been other men since, who had held her in their arms and kissed her—but not in the same way, never in the same way? They were like shadow figures now, Hugh, Richard and the others. They had no reality any more.

'I'd better tell you about the arrangements here,' Straun went on formally. His eyes were on her, two points of silver light in the twilit room. 'Mrs Weedon runs the house and does the cooking, and does it very well. She has help from a couple of daily women, who come in from the village every weekday, and there's also a gardener, Albert Mott, who lives in the cottage at the end of the drive. He does any odd jobs that need doing around the place too. As you know, I manage the estate, and that keeps me pretty well fully occupied—it isn't just the home farm, but I've tenant farmers too, and own most of the cottages in the village where their workers live.'

'It all sounds rather feudal,' Verity said as he paused, and Struan gave her one of his sharp glances.

'Yes, it probably does, but I try to run things on modern lines. I consider it a responsibility to see that everyone is treated properly. I have a farm manager and various other people to help me—the estate offices are nearby, purpose-built. Anyway, what I'm trying to tell you is that I don't have a lot of free time. I try to see as much as I can of Lucy, but I'm gone before she's awake in the morning—that's when she hasn't slipped out on one of these early expeditions of hers—and often still working when she goes to bed. I do try to get in for lunch, and for her tea-time at about five, but during the week that's about all. I manage more at weekends usually. He stopped again, and Verity wondered whether he was telling her why he wouldn't be seeing much of her too. 'That's why I'm concerned to see that she has continuity in her life.'

Verity hesitated. There was something about Straun that seemed to preclude personal questions, but she had to know—and surely as Lucy's nanny, even if only temporarily, she ought to. 'What about Gina?' she asked. 'Does—does she come here at all, or does Lucy go to her? Does she have access?'

Struan said nothing for a moment. Then he got up and walked over to the window. He stood with his back to her, a huge silhouette against the pale evening sky. Verity felt her heart quicken. Whatever he was about to say was important—to her, as well as to him and Lucy. There was a key here to the strange, oppressive feeling she had noticed in the house, to the brooding quality of its silence once Lucy had gone to bed, to the haunted look in Struan's eyes. She held her breath and waited.

'Gina's been away for quite a while,' Struan said at last. He turned and looked at her, but his face was so heavily shadowed that Verity could see nothing but the gleam of his eyes. In a low voice, he added, 'I'm not even sure that Lucy really remembers her at all well.'

'That's that, then,' Mrs Weedon declared, putting the final touches to an iced sponge and wrapping it in clear film before sliding it into the freezer. 'Enough meals to keep you going if you don't want to do any cooking, and plenty of meat and vegetables if you do. Mrs Tandy will do any preparation that's needed, so you don't need to be bothering yourself with that—just tell her in the mornings what you want. There's cakes and puddings ready too, and plenty of bread baked. Now, is there anything I've forgotten . . .?'

'I shouldn't think there could be—you've left us enough food to withstand a siege.' Verity looked at the freezer which Mrs Weedon had filled with food in preparation for her holiday. 'I think Mr Courtney ought to give you a bonus for doing all that—you're not having a holiday at all, just time in lieu for all the work you've done in advance! I hope he appreciates it.'

'Oh yes, he's very generous. He'd get in a temporary cook, but I couldn't be doing with anyone strange in my kitchen. We tried it once, and it was weeks before I found some of my pans and bowls, they'd all been changed round and never put back right, and the state of the fridge had to be seen to be believed! No, I'd sooner do it this way, so long as you don't mind, Miss Verity. I know it makes a bit extra for you, having to heat it up and so on.'

'I don't mind a bit. And I'll probably cook a few meals myself, if that's all right with you. And if Lucy gives me time!' Verity smiled wryly, still secretly amazed at the success she'd had with Lucy, who had attached herself firmly to her new nanny and spent every possible moment with her. It had been gratifying to have made such an impact on Struan's daughter, but it hadn't given Verity much opportunity to get to know Struan himself.

Not that she felt she needed to—hadn't she loved him for five years? But she knew, all the same, that although they had seemed to share a bond that was closer than any other she had ever experienced, there must be large areas in which they were still strangers. People could change in five years, their tastes and habits could alter. Everyday things like the soap he used, the books he read now, the music he liked—once, she had known these things, but now they were unknown territory to her, and a territory she was almost afraid to chart. Suppose she found that they had little in common after all?

Well, then, I'll know it's all been imagination, she told herself robustly. And it could be the best thing that could happen. I'll be able to leave Courtneys with a whole heart again.

Meanwhile, the process of finding out was clearly going to take some time—and not only because Struan rarely seemed to be indoors.

Being nanny to a lively five-year-old was, Verity had quickly discovered, a full-time and exhausting job. Her previous experience as an au pair had been with a family who wanted someone to help with the children while they were on holiday, and Verity's task had been to keep three small children amused on beaches in Spain and Greece, with the help of their mother, and to baby-sit during the evenings. She had never been left alone with the children for long periods as she was now.

Lucy proved to be an intelligent child, with an overwhelming curiosity. She began to ask questions as soon as she woke in the morning, and continued until falling asleep at night. It was fascinating, Verity found, to watch the development of her mind, and some of the conversations they had were quite profound. But in order to keep up with Lucy's quicksilver thoughts, Verity had to be alert all the time, and by the end of the first week she was reflecting ruefully that this must be what it was like to be on the other end of one of her own interviews. She wondered whether the celebrities she talked to felt as drained as this after she had left.

Struan was busy during that first week and, as he had warned Verity, she saw little of him—which was, she decided, probably just as well. If she was going to do this job, even temporarily, it had to be done properly, and she had no intention of letting Lucy suffer. Her confused feelings about Struan, and her need to sort them and herself out in order to be able to take up her own life again, must not be allowed to affect the child.

Mrs Weedon seemed as pleased as anyone to have her there. Not having a nanny for Lucy would have made it difficult for her to go ahead with her own holiday plans, and she had been afraid she might have to cancel them. Normally, she told Verity, it wouldn't have mattered—she always spent the fortnight with her sister, usually at her home in Torquay. But this year they'd decided to splash out and had booked a package holiday in Majorca. 'We'd have lost all the fare and everything if we'd cancelled at this short notice,' Mrs Weedon said. 'So it's a real blessing that you said you'd help out. And with Mr Courtney having known you when you lived here before, it's saved him having to get references—very strict about references, Mr Courtney is as a rule.' Clearly, she had no idea that there had been any but the most casual relationship between Verity and Struan, and for this Verity was thankful. If Mrs Weedon hadn't known, she reflected, it was unlikely that anyone else had either.

Mrs Weedon's holiday began next morning, and Struan himself drove her to the station to catch an early train. He was back in time to have breakfast with Lucy and Verity. Their first breakfast together, Verity thought as she sat opposite him in the little conservatory that was used as a breakfast-room. Close to the kitchen, it caught the morning sun, and was filled with green and flowering plants. How many breakfasts would they share here? she wondered, and determined to save as many memories as possible. They were going to have to last her a long, long time.

'Verry!' Lucy complained, jerking her out of her

thoughts. 'You're not listening. You're *miles* away. Daddy wants to take us out for a picnic.'

Verity came back to earth with a bump. How was she going to have any memories to save if she spent all her time dreaming? 'A picnic?' she echoed. 'That sounds lovely. Where?' Her mind raced. Did Struan really intend taking her and Lucy out for a day? A whole day—it sounded like paradise. But wasn't there peril in paradise?

'I thought you ought to see something of the Cotswolds while you're here,' Struan explained. 'I don't think you had much time for sightseeing when you lived here with your father.' Verity caught his glance and looked away, remembering those hot, timeless days when she had wandered in the fields and woods with Struan, content to be anywhere so long as it was with him. She had never been able to leave her father for very long, able only to snatch the odd afternoon or evening with Struan, but it had been enough. Neither of them had ever wanted to go farther afield.

Perhaps it was a measure of their changed relationship that Struan could suggest it now, she thought, and again didn't know whether to be glad or sorry. If only we could go back, she thought yearningly, go back to the love we had—the love I *thought* we had—then. If only we could pick it up again and go on from there ... But that was impossible. Struan had let her down in the cruellest way imaginable and she would be a fool to trust him again, even if he did care for her—which he obviously didn't. It was her bad luck that in spite of that, her feelings hadn't changed, that she still felt that curl of excitement, that hot flood of longing, whenever she looked at him. But perhaps a few weeks spent living in his house, looking after his daughter, would cure her of that. And meanwhile he must never know how she felt.

She glanced again in Struan's direction. He was looking at Lucy now, saying something to her, and she was able to study him without his noticing. He was looking fresh and casual this morning, in clean, well-cut jeans and a white shirt that showed off his deep tan. In the open neck, Verity could see the tangle of hairs that lay curled against his chest. They were as dark as the hairs that covered his bare arms, glinting in the sun as the muscles moved beneath them. 'You've been here a week and not had a day off yet,' he remarked. 'I daresay you'd like to get out for a few hours.'

His eyes met hers, cool and light, but was she imagining some deeper expression behind them, some darkness of emotion? Her heart kicked. Didn't he realise the dangers in spending a day with her, even with Lucy as a chaperon? He'd dismissed the attraction between them as nothing but physical desire—lust, to put it more crudely. But that didn't mean that it couldn't flare up all over again. Or had five years killed it?

Maybe that was in fact how he saw it. Maybe there really wasn't any danger—to him. Only to Verity.

Well, I took that risk when I offered to stay, she thought, and smiled at him. 'I'd love to go out for a picnic. But can you really spare the time? Aren't you too busy?'

'Even I have to take time off occasionally,' he told her. 'And I've seen far too little of Lucy lately. And since I've had to make a late start anyway—well, I might as well make it the whole day. Now—can you have a picnic ready fairly soon, or shall we have a pub lunch somewhere? There are plenty of nice little places around the Cotswolds.'

'A picnic, a picnic!' Lucy clamoured, and Struan and Verity smiled at each other.

'A picnic it seems to be,' she said. 'I'll get it ready.

It's no trouble—Mrs Weedon left us well-provided with quiches and salads, and I can soon make a few sandwiches. Lucy, you can help me.' She glanced up in surprise as Struan fetched a tray and began to load it from the breakfast table. 'No, don't bother, I can do that.'

'Certainly you can, but I'm going to.' He carried the tray out to the kitchen and began to load the dishwasher. 'It's not exactly hard work, after all. I'll fetch the picnic things too.' He turned for the door of the utility room at the same moment as Verity, and they collided, their bodies coming together with an almost violent impact. As Verity staggered, Struan put out his hands and caught her.

For several moments, they stood together, quite still. Verity was aware of her heart pounding, of the roaring of blood in her ears. She could feel Struan's fingers tightening round her arms. His chest was hard against the softness of her breasts, moving against her with the rapidity of his own breathing. The warmth of his body radiated towards her and she could smell the fresh, male scent that belonged to him alone.

Struan let her go and moved away. He didn't look at her as he went on through the door, and Verity was conscious of the sting of the tears in her eyes as she too turned away to fetch bread and make sandwiches. For a moment, as they'd stood so close, she had been transported back five years ... But Struan hadn't reacted at all. He'd just held her, long enough for her to regain her balance, and then let her go. It hadn't meant a thing to him.

So what did you expect? she asked herself, savagely cutting cheese. Passionate kisses? Abandoned love-making right here in the kitchen?

No. In the week since she'd arrived here she'd seen little of the passionate, headstrong Struan she re-

membered from five years ago. She knew better now
than to expect sudden passion—he had himself far too
tightly under control.

Maybe that was what was wrong, she thought with a
sudden ache in her heart. Maybe he needed to let
himself go a little, to give himself up to the arms of a
woman.

Well, if he did, it wasn't likely to be Verity Sandison,
the girl he'd known as a gauche, uncertain teenager.
She'd been attractive to him then; as a poised and
mature woman, she obviously wasn't. Not in the least.

Once again, she had to remind herself that that was
all to the good.

'Where are we going, Daddy?' Lucy demanded as she
scrambled into the back seat of Struan's Porsche,
clutching the battered old blue teddy bear that
accompanied her everywhere. 'Are we going to see a
castle?'

'No, not today.' Struan slammed down the boot and
came round to the driver's seat, glancing at Verity to
see that she was comfortable and safely strapped in.
'Today we're going to the Cotswold Farm Park to see
the animals——' He was interrupted by squeals of
delight from Lucy. 'There should be quite a few young
ones just now,' he went on, raising his voice slightly.
'You sound rather like a young animal yourself, Lucy,
when you make that noise.'

'I am a young animal,' Lucy replied matter-of-factly,
and her father sighed and smiled.

'I know you are. I was thinking of something
different. A piglet, for instance. One of those
Tamworths they have that look like little brown dogs
rushing about.'

'Oh, I don't mind being one of those, they're nice,'
Lucy said approvingly, and began to make piglet noises.

'You seem to have been to this place before,' Verity observed as Struan started the car. 'Tell me what it is—what did you call it, a Farm Park? Is it all farm animals, then?'

'Yes, but not ordinary farm animals. Rare ones. Sheep and cows and pigs, and donkeys and goats and chickens, and all kinds.' Lucy sat back in her seat, evidently feeling that she'd explained enough, and Verity looked enquiringly at Struan.

'They all sound fairly ordinary to me.'

'No, Lucy's right, they're all rare ones. Rare breeds. There are several places like it now, dotted around the country—they're important because they form a "gene bank". They keep old breeds going, breeds of sheep or cattle or pig or whatever, that would have died out by now because farmers just don't use them any more. Fashion changes in farm animals just as in anything else—our taste for meat changes, or our feeding techniques, one breed becomes popular for some reason and the others are abandoned. But we may need them again one day—it might, for instance, be important to have a sheep that will survive on seaweed, a pig that produces a particular kind of bacon or a sheep that grows a certain kind of wool. By keeping the breeds going, the Farm Park ensures that the genes are still available, and we can interbreed if necessary to get an animal that has the qualities we may need.'

'Yes, I see. I'd never thought of that—of breeds dying out,' Verity said thoughtfully. 'I suppose it's quite important. But are people really interested—enough to go specially to see them?'

'Oh yes. The place gets very busy, especially at this time of year when the babies are about. And some of the breeds are very attractive and interesting to see. The Jacob sheep, for example, with their four horns and patchy coloured coats—it's supposed to be from their

wool that Joseph's "coat of many colours" was woven.
And the Chillingham white cattle—they're from the
wild herd in Northumberland. A lot of domestic fowl
you rarely see these days. Yes, you'll find there's
plenty to interest you.'

'And rabbits,' Lucy put in from behind.

'*And* rabbits,' Struan agreed with a smile of
resignation. 'In fact, we'll be lucky if we get past their
enclosure. Actually, it was on a visit to the Farm Park
that Lucy first discovered rabbits. It could have been
worse, I suppose—it might have been Highland cattle
that she took a fancy to.'

'Yes, it might,' Lucy agreed in thoughtful tones.
'Daddy, you know that big field with nothing in it near
the church——'

'*No*,' Struan said forcefully. 'Now, be quiet for a
while, Lucy, and look at the scenery. You don't want
your tongue to wear out before you get to Guiting
Power, do you?'

'*What* did you say?' Verity asked, and he laughed.

'Guiting Power. Spelt "Gui" and pronounced "Guy".
It's the village nearest the Farm Park. A typically
baffling Cotswold name, isn't it—the kind I always
think an author wouldn't dare make up for a story
because nobody would believe it.'

Verity laughed and agreed. They entered a small
village with narrow, winding roads, and Struan fell
silent as he negotiated for right of way with a farm
tractor. Lucy had taken her father's advice to look at
the scenery, and Verity did the same.

The Gloucestershire countryside was at its most
lush now, the lanes fringed with grass the brilliant
green of early summer after a wet spring, the hedges
frothing with hawthorn blossom. Where the hedgerows
gave way to the drystone walls of the higher
Cotswolds, the grey of the stones was softened by a

lacework of wild parsley, huge umbrellas of foaming flowerheads leaning across the roads to make them even more narrow. Newly-shorn sheep, looking oddly naked without their heavy winter fleeces, grazed in the fields, their still-woolly lambs clustering together in mischievous groups. Soon, Verity knew, they would have lost their endearing sense of humour and become as stolid as their mothers, forgetting the days when they had run races round the meadows or played king of the castle on grassy knolls. Young animals, she thought, were invariably enchanting, from lambs and piglets to humans. And they could all be equally infuriating, when they felt like it.

'Lucy's asleep,' she remarked, glancing over her shoulder.

'Yes, she always drops off after the first quarter of an hour. Make the most of it—once she wakes up, her tongue will be going nonstop for the rest of the day.' Struan gave Verity a sideways glance and grinned. 'This is a regular annual trip, to the Farm Park—it's Lucy's favourite place. She's certainly an animal-lover, though I hope she doesn't take a fancy to some strange breed of sheep or cattle—they can take a lot of looking after, and I've enough on my plate just at present.'

He fell silent again, his mouth a little grim, and Verity remained quiet too. What was he thinking of? she wondered. Gina, and their broken marriage? What had gone wrong there? she wondered. But unless Struan himself chose to tell her—which seemed unlikely—there was no way of knowing. Any more than she'd ever known why he had married Gina so suddenly in the first place. Except that Lucy was obviously on the way, she reminded herself, and felt a fresh wave of the pain that never seemed to grow any less whenever she remembered the shock of coming home after her father's death to find Struan on the point of marrying

another girl and saying that she was no more entitled to
an explanation than any other casual acquaintance.

It was the callousness of that remark that had hurt
her more than anything else. That, and the complete
dismissal of the love she'd believed they shared. And we
did share it, she thought now, passionately. You *did*
love me, Struan. I know you did. So—what went
wrong? Why couldn't you wait?

With a flash of insight, she knew that simply being
with Struan wasn't going to be enough. Until she knew
what had happened to change him while she had been
with her father in Portugal, until she knew why he had
turned to another woman, and what had gone wrong
subsequently, she would never be able to settle. Never
complete, in the phrase that was beginning to haunt
her, that 'unfinished business'.

She glanced at his profile as he concentrated on
driving the sleek grey Porsche through the narrow
lanes. He looked more relaxed this morning, as if he
had decided to take a holiday from his personal
anxieties as well as from the estate. The lines of worry
that she'd noticed round his eyes seemed to have
smoothed out, leaving him looking younger, almost
carefree. Perhaps this was what he needed, a few days
out with his daughter, enjoying simple pleasures
without pressure. Perhaps then, relaxed and un-
pressurised, he might tell her what had happened . . .
perhaps they could regain the sheer joyful com-
panionship that had once been all they needed. . . .

Verity closed her eyes, fighting down the upsurge of
longing that shook her at the thought. Just to be with
Struan . . . it would surely be 'paradise enow' as the
poet had said. She didn't need luxury, the grand house,
the opulent furnishings, the sleek, expensive car. She
just needed to be with him, to be free to love him, to
know that he loved her.

But you *don't* know that, do you? demanded a tiny, irritating voice somewhere inside her. You don't know that he loves you. All you know is that five years ago he wanted you—wanted you quite badly. For a few hours, for maybe a couple of days. And since then? He probably hasn't given you another thought!

No, he probably hasn't, she admitted reluctantly. There had been that moment of recognition when she first arrived at Courtneys—the odd flash of understanding since, when their eyes had met and seemed to communicate some message that was gone almost before she had known it. There had been that moment in the kitchen, when they'd collided and she had felt a jolt like an electric shock as he'd touched and held her. But no—she had no real reason to suppose that any of these tiny events had been anything more than her own wishful imagination.

And even less reason to suppose that they had meant anything at all to Struan.

It was late afternoon before they finally left the Farm Park and found somewhere to have their picnic tea— they'd eventually settled for a pub lunch, saving the sandwiches, sausage rolls and fruit cake to have beside a clear, shallow stream before beginning the drive home. Verity had been delighted with the little pub they'd found, and Lucy was in her element sitting in the flowery garden and feeding chaffinches and sparrows with crumbs. She could already identify quite a lot of wild birds, Verity discovered, and wondered whether it was Struan or Gina who had taught her. Somehow, remembering the brittle sophistication of the girl whom she had seen once in the village during those pain-filled days before the wedding, she couldn't believe that it had been Gina, and Verity wondered just what kind of farmer's wife Gina had been. Not that Struan was an ordinary farmer . . .

Stop it! she told herself severely. Speculation like this was futile. She broke a piece of French bread and gave it to Lucy to feed the birds who kept hopping near their table, and made up her mind just to enjoy what she had. The moment of *now*—that was all anyone had, after all. Try to capture it, to hold it like a jewelled picture in a crystal ball, ready to be taken out and looked at later on, when it was all she had left. And it would be enough too, she thought as they spent the afternoon strolling through the enclosures of the Farm Park, gazing at the different breeds of animal, laughing at the antics of the young ones, stroking and patting those that came near the fence to be pampered with special food. This day, which was turning out to be so happy and relaxed, spent with Struan at her side— already it was more than she'd dared to dream of. If it were all she was ever to have, wouldn't it be enough?

Afterwards, their picnic spread out on a rug under a dipping willow-tree, she lay back and stretched her arms luxuriously above her head. Lucy had wandered away, hoping to catch fish in a yogurt pot, and the only sound was the drowsy hum of bees in the long grass.

'You look very peaceful,' Struan said quietly, and Verity opened her eyes to see him leaning over her, disturbingly close, his eyes dark. Her heart jolted, and she felt the shock pulse through her veins. She let her eyes wander to his mouth; its grimness had vanished, leaving it tender, almost vulnerable.

'It's a peaceful place,' she said at random, her voice little more than a whisper.

'Yes, it is, isn't it?' His own voice was a sigh, as if he wistfully acknowledged that the peace could only be found here, that it wouldn't accompany them back to Courtneys. 'I sometimes think this is the real way to live—just doing nothing very much on a riverbank in the sun. And being with someone you—like.' The hesitation was infinitesimal, but Verity's sharpened senses picked it up. What had he been going to say? she wondered, and gathered up her courage.

'Even better with someone you love.'

Struan's eyes had wandered away, taking in the solitude of their picnic spot. They returned to her face with a quick flash that was instantly veiled.

'Someone you love. Yes, I suppose so—but how do you know who that is? How do you tell?'

Verity opened her mouth to say, *but surely that's easy*—then she paused. How *did* you tell? Had *she* been able to tell, with Hugh and Richard? She'd believed herself to be in love with them, but when the moment of truth had come she'd known that she wasn't. What happened if the moment of truth came too late?

Was that what happened with Struan and Gina?

'How do you tell?' Struan repeated, and his tone was urgent. 'How do you know when that person comes along—the one you love? The one you want to spend your life with? What happens to make it different from all the other encounters—the infatuations, the affairs? Or isn't there any difference at all?' His voice dropped, became wearily cynical. 'Maybe it's all a con after all. A trick of Nature to make us think we're in love, to make us go through all the complicated procedure that's necessary to keep the human species going. It's a pretty undignified process after all, when all's said and done, and if we didn't have this damned urge, this driving need, we probably wouldn't ever bother, and then where would the world be?' Verity, too shocked to speak, didn't answer, and after a moment he said bitterly, 'Probably a great deal better off, when you look at the despoliation of the planet man's managed to achieve so far.'

He was staring blindly at the river now, all his earlier contentment gone, and Verity put out her hand to him.

He started as she laid her fingers tentatively on his bare arm, and turned to look down at her, his eyes bewildered, almost as if he was wondering who she was and why she was there. For a few breathless moments, they stared at each other, Struan's eyes haunted with dark questions, Verity's burning with the need to communicate some kind of answer, some kind of comfort. But how could she comfort him when she didn't know what was wrong? What could she give him when she didn't know his need?

'Verity . . .' he muttered thickly, and she slid her hand up his arm, trembling as she felt the warm bare skin under her palm. She felt a shiver run from his body to hers, quivered with a sudden excitement that was totally beyond her control as Struan's fingers touched her face, tracing the lines of her cheek, her lips, her eyes. The bitterness of his expression had given way now to a wondering tenderness, the hard line of his mouth had softened, the silver of his eyes darkened with desire; and it was with a feeling of inevitability that Verity lifted her face and offered her lips to receive the kiss that had to come.

Both her arms were round his neck as he lowered himself over her, gently drawing him closer. It was like touching a wild animal, she thought with a tremor—too sudden a movement and he might shy away, be lost to her. But as their lips met, a shock of overwhelming sensation jolted through them both, a warm rush of longing that shook their bodies so that instinctively they clasped each other closer, the kiss that had begun so tentatively hardening to a mutual, almost savage demand. Verity felt Struan's lips, their softness giving way to a potency that was purely masculine, teasing hers apart, his tongue flicking against her mouth with a sensuality that brought from her a spontaneous and entirely intuitive response. Letting her own tongue meet his in joyous union, she raised her body against his, arching herself towards him so that her breasts, already tightening with the force of her body's yearning, thrust against the hardness of his chest. She could feel his warmth through the thin cotton of his shirt and the light silk of her own blouse, and when she let her hand stray down the throbbing column of his neck to the unfastened buttons her fingers tangled in the curling black hairs that she had glimpsed before.

Struan groaned somewhere deep in his throat. His hands were urgent now, moving over her body with a feverish haste as if he knew that there was little time, that sanity would all too soon return. Verity twisted in his arms, her body wanting to follow the seeking fingers, wanting to prolong the exquisite sensations that his touch evoked. His mouth had left hers, was travelling down her slender neck, thrusting aside the silky covering and flimsy lace that enclosed her breasts, smothering her flushed skin with tiny, passionate kisses that had her whimpering for more. Her mind was barely working now, all logical thought disrupted by a turmoil of confused impressions, a tumbling kaleidoscope of sensation, delight, desire; while her body was reacting to each new, unfamiliar experience with an instinct that was wholly primitive, and told her clearly just why it was that she had never been able to go even as far as this with any other man.

'Verity,' Struan muttered again, lifting his lips from her smooth breast, his eyes almost black now with only a silver edging like the glimmer of sun around a stormy cloud. 'My God, Verity—if only I'd—known—if only someone could have told me. . . .' His eyes searched hers with a desperation that caught at her heart and made her tighten her arms around him, drawing him down again to her breast where he fastened his lips on her hardened nipple like a hungry child. 'But it wouldn't have been any good——' she felt rather than heard the words that he ground out against her quivering skin '—it wouldn't have made any difference. It *couldn't*—God forgive me, I couldn't have done anything else——'

'Struan, don't!' Torn with a compassion that was almost as powerful as her desire, she lifted his face from her body and searched the tormented eyes. 'Forget it, Struan, whatever it is that's tearing you apart. Forget it for a little while at least—if this is all we can have, my darling, let's just have it, let's have something to keep, to remember, to look at when we're apart.' Her own eyes, sapphire-dark, burned into his. 'Love me, Struan,' she whispered, the world forgotten in the intensity of her need. 'Love me now—*please*.'

He stared down at her, and in that moment the communication between them was complete. It always had been, she discovered with a joy that burst within her like an opening rose. Whatever had happened in the five years that had parted them, even in the time before they had ever met, Struan was her man and she was his woman. Nothing—*nothing*—could change that. If they were wrenched apart at that moment and never met again, it would still hold true.

But they weren't going to be wrenched apart. They were together, completely and joyously together.

Struan lowered his face to hers again, brushing her lips with a featherlight touch that was almost unbearably exciting. Verity felt her body shudder in his arms, felt him gather her close, murmuring her name with a husky tenderness that seemed to reach down into her soul. He stretched his body against hers and she turned herself slightly to press close against him, acutely aware of each hardened contour. With infinite sensitivity, he ran his fingertips down the length of her body, from the soft lobe of her ear, down her neck, over the aching swell of her breast and the tingling of her stomach to her thigh, where they lingered sensuously. The arm that was still around her shoulders tightened, drawing her closer, and his lips began to increase their demands.

There was a sudden frantic splashing from nearby, and a shriek that seemed to split the breathless air.

'Lucy!'

They were apart instantly, scrambling up, dazed and shaken. With a rush of shame, Verity realised that they had forgotten all about the little girl, had let her wander off along the riverbank, had succumbed to their own driving passion without thought for what might happen to her—what she might see. Suppose she had come back, found them—but she hadn't. She had strayed along the grassy banks, fallen into the water, and was now crying for help, perhaps in real danger . . .

'It's all right.' Struan had reached his daughter while Verity was still floundering through the trailing branches of the willow trees, fingers shakily trying to fasten her blouse as she came. 'It's all right, Lucy, you're just wet, there's nothing wrong with you. What were you doing, trying to catch a fish? I don't think there are any, the water's too shallow.'

'It was a frog.' Lucy was standing on the bank, half-crying, half-laughing, trying to squeeze water from her soaked jeans. 'I'd almost got it and it jumped. I wanted to take it back for the pond.'

'Good lord, the pond's full of tadpoles, we'll have thousands of frogs without importing new ones. Here, dry your face with this.' Struan gave her his handkerchief. 'Feeling better? Let's go back to the picnic and dry you properly with the tea towel. Not that we can do much about those jeans, you'd better take them off.'

'But I've got nothing else to wear.' Lucy had stopped

shivering, and was treating the situation with her normal practical matter-of-factness. Verity felt suddenly unneeded; father and daughter seemed to have the matter well in hand, coping with perfect understanding, while she was still feeling sick at the thought of what might have happened. She looked at the two dark heads, the faces that were so absurdly alike in spite of the differences caused by Struan's haunted cragginess and Lucy's tender youth. A cold chill crept through her body, making her shiver as if it had been she who had fallen into the stream. How could she have forgotten that Struan had abandoned her to marry Lucy's mother; that by allowing him to make love to her she was merely paving again a road that she already knew led directly to hell? And that while she had been doing it, Lucy could have drowned . . .

'We'll wrap you up in the car rug,' Struan was telling Lucy now as he lifted her in his arms and carried her back to the spot where, only moments before, he and Verity had lain locked in passion. 'Come on, strip off those wet things while Verity and I pack up, and we'll get you home. Not that you're likely to catch cold on a day like this, is she, Verity?'

'No,' Verity summoned up the strength to answer. 'No, I shouldn't think so. It was just a swim, after all.' She began to collect together the picnic things, her hands shaking as she packed them into the basket. Struan shook out the rug on which they'd been sitting, picked off a few bits of grass, and wrapped it round Lucy's slim, naked body.

'There,' he said, lifting her into the car and settling her on the back seat. 'Snug as a bug in a rug.' He came back to Verity and looked down at her, his eyes dark with concern. 'Are you all right?'

'Yes—just a bit shaken.' She forced herself to meet his eyes. What must he be feeling now—remorse, shame, disgust? 'Lucy—she could have drowned . . .'

'That's not very likely.' Struan's voice was gentle. 'The stream's only inches deep and she wasn't far away. But I know what you mean. We'd rather forgotten she was around, hadn't we?' He smiled at her and she felt comforted, knowing that he wasn't blaming her for what had happened. 'Verity,' he went on, and his voice had changed now, become more intense, 'we've got to talk. There are things——'

'You don't have to tell me,' she interrupted. There *were* things that stood between them, she knew that, and only a few hours earlier she'd said to herself that until she knew what they were she could have no peace of mind. But how could she trust Struan to tell her the truth? He'd refused all those years ago; now that he wanted her again, would he tell her what had happened, truthfully, leaving nothing out however damning? Or would it be an edited version, worded so as to gain her sympathy—though she couldn't imagine how—so that he could at last assuage the desire he felt for her? Which was, she reminded herself yet again, in his own words— *no more than physical*.

It might even be the best thing that could happen, she thought wryly. Going to bed with Struan, allowing him to make love to her, might be just what she needed to wipe him from her heart. But even as the thought crossed her mind, she knew that it wouldn't work. Because it was lust only on Struan's side. For her, it was, quite definitely and hopelessly, love. And giving herself to him would only root it more deeply in her heart. Once give way, she thought defeatedly, and she would never be able to cut free. 'You don't have to tell me anything,' she finished lamely. 'I—I'm not sure I want to know.'

He watched her for a moment, a momentary bafflement in his eyes before his expression closed again. He opened his mouth to speak, but Verity turned away; and when he touched her she moved abruptly so that his hand fell back.

'Let's go, shall we?' she said with a forced brightness. 'Poor Lucy's had a long day, and now she's sitting in the car with nothing on but a rather tickly rug. Let's get her home and into bed.'

'And after that?' he persisted, his eyes darkly intent.

'After that? Well, I suppose one of Mrs Weedon's suppers.' The pain was like a knife twisting in her heart as she walked ahead of him to the car and slid into the passenger seat. After that, she knew, Struan would be all too willing to take up where they had left off. And that couldn't be allowed. It could only make her own problems and his—whatever they were—worse; could only make Lucy's life more insecure.

It came as a shock to Verity to realise just how much Lucy herself mattered in all this. She had only known the child for a few weeks, yet already the small fingers had twined themselves round her heart. If it had just been Struan and me, she thought miserably, everything would have been so simple. But there are too many people who could get hurt; too many complications.

What had happened on the riverbank must never be allowed to happen again.

CHAPTER SIX

VERITY and Lucy were having their tea in the garden when Jamie Kenwood arrived. It was a moment or two before she recognised him; then her mind flashed back, with the inevitable accompanying stab of pain, to the day she had come home from Portugal. It had been Jamie who came to meet her; Jamie who had, unknowingly, broken the news of Struan's betrayal . . .

'Dr Kenwood!' she exclaimed, jumping up to greet him. 'How nice to see you. I don't suppose you remember me, though. Verity Sandison.' He had been one of the people she had been looking forward to meeting again when she came back to Lane End—the first on her list, she remembered, though that seemed an age ago now. And she had gone along to his surgery, only to find that he was away on a course and a strange locum was there in his place.

'Indeed I do.' The brown eyes regarded her with warm admiration. 'Although I must say you look rather different from the shy little teenager who used to live at Lane End. Quite a transformation, in fact!'

Verity blushed and laughed. 'I'm sure I don't look very sophisticated in these clothes,' she disclaimed, looking down at the brief yellow shorts and bikini top which were all she was wearing. Her skin had tanned to a soft honey-gold during the fine weather, and the sun had bleached her blonde hair several shades paler, making her eyes look startlingly blue in contrast.

'It's not the clothes, and I didn't mention sophistication – although I'm sure you have plenty of that when you choose.' Jamie studied her thoughtfully. 'No, it's a maturity that shows in your eyes, the way you hold your head, your entire bearing. You've turned into a beautiful woman, Verity, do you know that?'

Verity blinked, and Jamie Kenwood laughed. 'Don't worry, I'm not really such a fast worker as that makes me sound! It's a purely objective statement, but none the less valid for that—I hope I haven't offended you.'

'No, of course not—I should have remembered that you come straight to the point.' Verity indicated a white wrought-iron chair. 'Would you like some tea? There's plenty here. Lucy, fetch Dr Kenwood a cup.'

'He can use Daddy's,' Lucy said. 'Daddy won't be coming now. He told me he might be going over to Holloways.'

'Oh.' Verity felt deflated. Since the day of the picnic, tea had been the only meal she had shared with Struan—he had been out, or coming in late, each evening, and they had seen little of one another. It had been partly her own doing, she knew—when they had come back after Lucy's wetting she had hurried the child upstairs to her bath and deliberately avoided Struan, leaving his meal ready for him in the dining-room and carrying her own upstairs. It had been a long, tense evening as she sat at the window in the gathering dusk, wondering if he would come to find her, not sure whether or not she wanted him to. But he hadn't come. Hours later, she'd heard his footsteps on the stairs and had felt her body tighten, but they had turned away towards his own room and there had been no more sounds.

Since then, they seemed to be carrying out some mutual, unspoken agreement that it was better if they didn't meet alone. As usual, Struan was out of the house by the time she and Lucy came down for breakfast, taking a packed lunch to eat in the fields or perhaps calling in at the village pub for a snack. In the afternoons he usually dropped in as they were having tea, and after a short time Verity would make some excuse and leave father and daughter together, unable to bear the questioning darkness of his eyes. She spent the evenings in her room, near Lucy, fighting down the desperate longing to go to him, to let the desire that was so near the surface carry them both into the world of rapturous oblivion that she knew existed somewhere for them to share. But she dared not do it. They were, she knew, very near the point of no return, and past it lay forbidden, and dangerous, territory.

Lucy's voice jerked her back to the present, and she blinked again at the man who sat opposite her under the yellow sun umbrella. Friendly brown eyes, twinkling in a cheerful face, a mouth that smiled easily, an expression that was easy to read ... Guiltily, she realised that he was waiting for her to pour his tea, and she hastily pulled herself together and lifted the pot.

'Sorry, I was thinking of something else for a minute,' she apologised. 'How do you like it, Dr Kenwood? It's got rather strong, but I can add some hot water if you——'

'No, it's fine like that.' Jamie took the cup and gave her a quizzical look. 'What's all this "Dr Kenwood" stuff? Even as a shy teenager you managed to call me Jamie.'

'Yes—I did, didn't I?' Verity relaxed suddenly and smiled at him. 'Let's start again. How *are* you, Jamie? What's been happening to you in the past five years? Are you married?'

'No, not yet. Haven't found the right girl, or maybe no woman would put up with me. A doctor's hours aren't very social, and a lot of young doctors marry nurses they meet during their hospital years—nurses understand the job, you see. Didn't happen to me, so here I am, still unattached.' He glanced at Verity's hand as she passed him a plate of buttered scones. 'I can't believe that you are, too.'

'And why not?' she challenged him. 'Modern girls don't get married the moment they leave school, you know. We have interesting jobs, careers. Men have to offer rather more than a home and a pile of nappies these days.'

'But that seems to be just what you've opted for anyway, except that it's someone else's home and nappies,' he pointed out, and Verity caught herself up short. Clearly, Jamie was under the impression that she was a full-time nanny, and until Struan himself knew the truth about her career it would probably be better if he went on thinking that way. But before she could reply, Lucy had interrupted with the indignant remark that she didn't wear nappies, she wasn't a *baby*.

'I had to come home with nothing on the other day, though,' she informed Jamie, her mouth full of scone. 'I was a bug in a rug, wasn't I, Verry?'

'You certainly were.' Verity gave Jamie a wry glance. 'I don't think she'd ever heard that expression before, and she's been driving us mad with it ever since.'

'It was an adventure,' Lucy said indistinctly.

'Yes, but you don't have to spray crumbs all over us to tell us about it,' Verity told her. 'Don't talk with your mouth full, Lucy, wait until you've finished before you speak.'

'But then I'll want to say something else.'

'Well, it can't be helped. It's good manners.' Verity repressed a smile at Lucy's mutinous expression and turned back to Jamie. 'Did you want to see Struan? It sounds as though he won't be back until late, if he's gone to Holloways. That's the farm over the hill, isn't it?'

'Yes, and he's on good terms with Mike Holloway and his wife, so he'll quite probably stay to supper. It doesn't matter, I didn't want to see him about anything in particular—just dropped in. And of course I wanted to see you.' He grinned at her. 'The village grapevine is buzzing with news of the latest nanny, didn't you know?'

'Gossip?' Verity said lightly, though her heart was thumping uncomfortably. What were they saying? The village would know all about Straun and Gina's divorce —what interpretation were they putting on her presence here?

But Jamie shook his head. 'Not really, no, just friendly interest in the main. Don't forget, they're nearly all employees of Struan's themselves, so naturally they're interested. And Struan wouldn't stand for gossip of any kind—he's always been hypersensitive about that kind of thing. I suppose it was the experiences the family went through with Justin that caused that—he was hardly ever out of the gossip columns with his wild exploits, and Struan has shunned the limelight ever since.'

'I see.' Once again, Verity wished that she'd told Struan at the outset that she was a journalist. But then he would never have asked her to stay, never have taken her on as Lucy's nanny, even temporarily, and she would have had to leave without having even this short time with him.

And wouldn't that have been better all round? her mind asked coldly. Wouldn't it have saved a great deal of pain?

She looked thoughtfully at Jamie, who was now chatting with Lucy, listening with real interest as she described the latest exploits of Mr and Mrs Macgregor. He was a nice man, she thought, remembering the way he'd cared for her father, comforted her when he'd died. The sort of man you could trust. The sort of man you could confide in.

Could she confide in him now? Would it help?

But there wasn't really all that much to tell, was there? Only a summer romance five years ago, an encounter that had seemed to mean so much but might have meant nothing at all. And a silent recognition now that, for her, nothing had changed—that she loved Struan hopelessly and completely, and didn't expect ever to stop.

But that was all she knew. She didn't really know about Struan. Oh, he'd kissed her on the riverbank the other day, and she knew that he'd wanted then— perhaps still wanted—to make love to her. But wasn't that simply a result of his own deep unhappiness and frustration—an unhappiness and frustration that had come about solely because of his divorce?

If it were, then Verity had been right to avoid him. She mustn't allow anything to happen that he might regret—that might add a deep, burning remorse to the torment he was already suffering. Because, even through her own bitterness, she had to acknowledge that, cruelly though he had treated her, he had stopped short of the ultimate cruelty. He could so easily have taken the love she had innocently offered him, used her body to assuage the desire he'd still felt for her. She remembered the savage torture that had ravaged his face on that last day. He'd wanted her then. He could have taken her—but he hadn't. For that, at least, she could thank him. But for his own sake as well as hers, it was as vital that it shouldn't happen now—five years too late for them both.

'You're looking very thoughtful,' Jamie said gently, and she started a little. 'Is anything wrong?'

'Oh—no, nothing really.' She tried a bright smile that didn't feel quite right. 'I was just letting my mind wander, I'm afraid. Lucy, if you've finished you can get down. What are you going to do now?'

'Feed the Macgregors. I collected all those dandelions
and things, didn't I? D'you want to come, Jamie?'

'I will when I've finished my tea,' he said, smiling at
her, and she nodded and ran off. Verity refilled his cup.

'She's a bright little thing,' he observed, spreading
Mrs Weedon's home-made strawberry jam on a scone.
'You get on well with her, don't you?'

'Yes. I've grown very fond of her since I've been here.
And I feel sorry for her, too. She seems so—well, lost,
in a way. I suppose it's because she misses her mother.'

Jamie gave her another thoughtful look, but didn't
volunteer any information. You could hardly expect
him to, Verity thought, slightly ashamed of herself for
trying to lead the conversation in that direction. He was
Struan's best friend and had probably been Gina's
doctor. If anyone knew the truth, it would be Jamie,
and he could never tell.

'You seem a little lost yourself,' he said, surprising
her. 'There's an anxious look in your eyes—it's making
tiny lines on that smooth brow which oughtn't to be
there at your age.' He paused, then added quietly, 'You
once agreed to look on me as a friend, Verity. That still
holds. If there *is* anything wrong—anything you need to
talk about—well, don't hesitate to come to me.
Sometimes just having someone to talk to is enough. A
friendly, listening ear.'

Verity looked up into his eyes. They were a dark,
warm brown, full of kindly concern. The urge to
confide in him was very strong. He was right—a
listening ear would make all the difference. If she could
only pour out the confused turmoil of thoughts, of
hopes and fears, of desolate loneliness—wouldn't it
make things easier to bear? Wouldn't it help her to sort
herself out, to know what she must do?

She took a deep breath and leaned forward.

'Verry! Verry! Look who's here!' Verity jerked

upright again, twisting in her seat to see Lucy
scampering across the lawn, followed by a tall, familiar
figure—a figure of whom the very sight set her pulses
racing. 'Daddy's come home after all,' Lucy went on
unnecessarily. 'Isn't it lovely? I'll go and get another
cup, Daddy—Jamie's used yours.'

'And drunk all your tea and eaten your scones and
cake as well, I'm afraid,' Jamie remarked, not looking
in the least penitent. 'Jolly good they were, too.'

'I'll go and fetch some more.' Verity got hastily to her
feet, feeling flustered and shaken. Why did the sudden,
unexpected sight of Struan have to affect her like this?
She could feel his eyes on the colour in her cheeks, and
knew that this was only making them worse. She began
hurriedly to load the tray.

'It doesn't matter, I had tea at Holloways.' Struan's
eyes were still on her, as bright and cold as winter stars.
'Did you come to see me about anything special,
Jamie?'

'Not really, though I did want to have a chat about
one small matter.' Verity caught Struan's eyes on her
and felt her blush deepen even more. Clearly, he was
telling her to go, to leave him and Jamie in private. She
muttered something, picked up the tray and walked
across the lawn towards the house. She could feel the
silvery brightness of Struan's eyes on her back all the
way.

What was the matter with him? Was he regretting
ever having asked her to stay? Was he going to tell her
next that he'd found another nanny for Lucy, that he'd
decided not to wait for Miss Morris, and that she was
dismissed?

Her heart chilled as she thought of it. It would have
been hard enough to have left Courtneys that first
morning, knowing that she would never see Struan
again. It would be infinitely harder now—now that she

knew just how deeply she loved him. And now that she loved Lucy too.

Verity didn't see Struan again until she was putting Lucy to bed later that evening. Lucy, as usual, was engrossed in a conversation about the Macgregor family; while she had been showing them to Jamie, one of the younger Macgregors had escaped from the hutch and involved them in a furious chase round the garden before he could be caught. This had given Lucy the idea of organising rabbit races, and she was trying to work out how it could be done.

'I honestly don't think it would work,' Verity said as she folded clothes and wondered what Lucy did to her jeans to get such large holes in the knees. Most of them now were adorned with brightly-coloured patches. 'You'd lose half of them.' Which might, she thought privately, be quite a good thing, although Struan might not think so when they got into his crops.

At that moment, Struan appeared in the doorway. Verity gave him a quick glance and turned away from the ice in his eyes. What *had* she done? Was there gossip in the village after all, in spite of what Jamie had said, and had he heard it? Did he think she might have started it herself—trying to compromise him in some way? It seemed fantastic, but there must be some explanation for that chilling expression.

'Oh, Daddy!' Lucy was sitting up in bed, her eyes bright. 'Daddy, we're going to have rabbit races in the garden, all the Macgregors running against each other, and Jamie says you have to have a book, only I don't know what sort of book to have. Is it a prize? Do you know what kind of book it ought to be? Verity doesn't.'

'*Peter Rabbit*, I should think,' her father said dryly. 'And whose brilliant idea was this?' He came into the room and sat on Lucy's bed.

'Mine, of course.' Lucy was quite unaware of any irony in his tone. 'You'll come, though, won't you? When we have the races?'

'I think you'd better organise them first. You'll need plenty of fencing, to stop them getting away.' Verity watched in astonishment as he produced a paper and pencil and began to write. 'And then they'll all need special feeding, to build up their strength. And practice gallops every morning, as they do with horses—that has to be very early, around five o'clock. You'll need racecards too, and stands, and——' He wrote busily and with complete solemnity, while Lucy began to look doubtful. 'Let's see, what else is there—you'll have to fence off part of it for a winner's enclosure, that's essential—it's going to be a lot of work, I'm afraid, and just at present I'm too busy to help. But once you've got it organised I'll come, of course. I'm looking forward to it already.' He stopped writing and gazed at his daughter.

'I wasn't really thinking of anything like that,' she began uncertainly. 'I just thought we could make them all run for a—a dandelion, or a lettuce or something. I don't think they'd like real racing. Actually, I don't think they'd like racing at all.'

'No, I expect you're right about that,' Struan agreed, closing his notebook. 'Rabbits are probably happier just being rabbits. Anyway, we needn't think any more about it now, it's time to go to sleep. Does Verity read to you?'

'Yes. We're doing *Watership Down*.' Lucy snuggled down under the sheets, her own eyes as bright as a small animal's. 'You can do it tonight if you like, Daddy.'

'That's just what I was about to suggest.' He took the book Verity handed him and blinked. 'Good heavens, are you really wading through this tome? Isn't it a bit old?'

'It's about rabbits,' Verity told him, and he nodded resignedly. 'I don't read it all—we skip the dull bits. But if you'd rather read something else——'

'No, no, this is fine. You go on down and find something to eat, I'll see that Lucy's all right.' He stood up and followed Verity to the door, and she saw that his eyes were dark, a glimmering pewter grey in the dusk of Lucy's shaded room. 'We'll eat together tonight, Verity, if you don't mind. No sneaking off to your room, all right? I want to talk to you.'

'Yes,' she said, her mouth almost too dry to form the word. So this was it. Struan clearly meant to dismiss her. He had decided, for whatever reason, that he could no longer have her in the same house.

Within a short time—perhaps by tomorrow—this strange existence would be over. It had been a mixture of pain and pleasure. The delight of getting to know Lucy; the heady desire she'd felt in Struan's arms; the thrilling rapture of knowing that he wanted her too. And the pain of knowing that they could never be truly together, a pain that was more bitter than anything she had ever known—even crueller than the pain of his betrayal.

And it would be nothing, she knew, when compared with the agony of having to leave.

'Mrs Weedon certainly made sure we'd be well fed,' Struan remarked as he came into the dining-room half an hour later to find Verity setting plates on the table. 'Is that her *chicken suprême*? One of my favourites.'

The words were ordinary enough, but his voice sounded slightly clipped, as if he were keeping himself tightly under control. Verity gave him a cautious glance, afraid of the ice that had been in his eyes earlier, but his expression was shuttered and unreadable. He went across to the sideboard.

'I thought we might have a bottle of wine, to celebrate.'

'Celebrate?' Verity's voice came out huskily, ending on a squeak. She bit her lip, wishing she'd said nothing. What was he trying to do to her?

'Celebrate having a meal together again. It seems a long time.' He found the corkscrew and began to draw the cork. 'We seem to have been circling round each other like a pair of wary dogs, don't we?'

'Do we? I—I hadn't noticed.'

'Of course you had.' Struan poured wine into a glass and tasted it. 'Hm. Not bad at all. You'll have some?' He filled a glass and set it beside her before coming back to the table with his own. 'Wine does help, after all, doesn't it? To relax people. To loosen the tongue.'

If anyone needed relaxing, Verity thought, it was Struan himself. His tall body looked as taut as a spring, each muscle and sinew as ready for action as if he'd been a tiger stalking his prey. The effect of some powerful jungle animal was enhanced by the narrow black trousers that fitted his thighs like a second skin, and by the sleek black cashmere pullover. He looked sinister—menacing . . .

And that's what he was, Verity thought with a catch of fear in her throat. A menace. A threat to my peace of mind, to my whole life. It would have been better for me—better, maybe, for us both—if we'd never met . . .

They began to eat in silence. Verity picked at her food. The chicken dish was delicious, yet somehow its flavour paled and disappeared as she tried to eat. She pushed it away and fetched the dessert. It was blackcurrant cheesecake, the fruit sharp in contrast to the creaminess of the filling, but after the first few mouthfuls she found it uninteresting and bland.

'You don't seem to be very hungry,' Struan observed. 'Drink your wine, at least.'

'So that I relax?' she asked in a brittle voice. 'And then what?'

'Then nothing, of course. Did you think I was trying to get you drunk—so that I could have my wicked way with you?' His voice was harsh, and she raised startled sapphire eyes. 'Is there any reason why I should think that necessary?'

It took Verity a moment or two to understand his meaning. She gasped. 'Just what are you getting at?'

'Well, it isn't, is it?' His eyes were almost black, outlined with only a narrow rim of silver that gave them a strange, alien look which frightened her. 'Necessary, I mean. After all, you didn't need drink the other afternoon, down by the river. Nor today, with Jamie.' He added the last words in a low voice, as if it hurt to say them, while Verity gazed at him in consternation.

'I don't know what you mean,' she whispered. 'There was nothing happening between Jamie and me—we were just talking——'

'Were you? It looked like a very intimate discussion to me.' His voice was bitter, and Verity remembered that she had indeed been leaning forward, about to confide in Jamie, as Struan had appeared. 'I suppose you'll be telling me next that Jamie wasn't the reason why you came back to Lane End.'

'*Jamie* the reason why I—no, of course he wasn't!' Verity bit off the next words that had so nearly been shocked out of her—that Struan himself was the reason. 'I haven't even seen him for five years—I'd almost forgotten him.'

'Had you?' Struan gave her that brooding look, then stood up abruptly. Without warning, he grasped at her wrist and jerked her to her feet, pulling her close to him. 'Had you really? Well, maybe you had at that. Maybe

you've been too busy during these past few years—busy
with other men. Is that it?' He glared down into her
eyes, his own smouldering like brands that needed little
to set them alight again. Quickly, he transferred both
her wrists to one of his powerful hands, leaving the
other one free to roam over her back, cupping her small
bottom to hold her firmly against him. 'How many men
have there been in the last five years?' he muttered, his
lips brushing hers, and she quivered with a wild
sensation that was part excitement, part fear. 'Just how
far have you come from that shy, unawakened teenager
who went walking in the fields with me?'

Verity felt the treacherous weakness of her legs,
threatening to give way under her. She closed her eyes,
fighting the desire that surged through her body,
tingling in her stomach and thighs, aching in her limbs.
If only she could let herself go, let her body mould itself
to his, let all the pent-up love and passion come pouring
out. But she dared not risk it. There was an anger in
Struan tonight that she didn't understand, a furious
rage that could all too easily turn to cruelty. And
would, afterwards, leave them both shaken and
changed, unable ever to go back.

'How many?' he insisted, his lips still teasing hers.

'Please——' she implored him. 'Struan, please—let
me go, I beg you. There haven't been any men—none
who mattered——'

'So they don't even have to matter! You just use them
to amuse yourself, is that it? The modern woman—
sleeping around for the fun of it, not letting anyone get
to her heart. My God, you disgust me!' He held her
away from him, his mouth curling with scorn. 'And you
don't even care, do you? It's just a game to you—
another heart to pin up like a poor, struggling fly,
another scalp to hang on your belt before you go on to
the next one. Where do you think you'll end up, Verity?

In the bed of some rich man who'll take you on for life and close his eyes to your fun and games? Or lonely and embittered, wondering why nobody loves you any more?'

The tears spilled from Verity's eyes as she stared up at the cold, implacable face. This wasn't Struan talking—it couldn't be. It was some other being who was inhabiting his body, some tortured soul who was flailing around its cage in desperation, battering at every wall in the hope of finding a way out.

'Struan, please listen. It's not like that at all. I don't sleep around, I never have—I've never even slept with one man. Yes, there have been men who wanted to—there have been men who wanted to *marry* me. But I couldn't say yes. I never could. That——' she took a deep breath '—that's why I came here. To see you.'

Struan stared at her. His burning eyes searched her face. His expression began to change, from scorn to disbelief; and then, slowly, to a cautious, wondering hope. As if his fingers had been too tightly cramped to move quickly, he released her wrists. One hand drew her close again while the other travelled slowly up to her face, tilting it towards him, the fingers gently caressing away the tears.

'To—see—me?' he repeated, his voice husky.

Verity nodded. 'I've never forgotten you,' she whispered brokenly. 'That day just before you were married—it went somewhere very deep in me. It was as if whatever feelings I had were frozen from that moment on, locked up somewhere inside me. As if I could never feel anything for any other man—only you.' She took a deep breath, knowing that she was at the point of no return. Once she had exposed her deepest, most vulnerable emotions to Struan, there could be no drawing back. She had ceased to listen to

rational thought and was working now purely from
instinct—an instinct that could lead her to a deeper
humiliation, a more cruel hurt even than she had
already known, but which had to have its way. 'I had to
find out what it meant—whether it was real. It was
affecting my life—I wanted to love someone, but I
could never commit myself. I had to come back to—
to——' She shrugged, unable to continue.

'Did you know about the divorce?' he asked quietly,
and Verity shook her head.

'No. It wasn't like that, Struan. I didn't want to
break up your marriage. I didn't want to start an affair,
or anything like that. I just knew that if I were ever to
be free of you, I had to come back to Lane End, where
it all happened. I'm not sure that I even intended to see
you again. I just had to be here—to get you out of my
system.' She glanced up, afraid that she had hurt him.
His face was grave.

'And?'

'It didn't work,' she admitted honestly. 'I realised
that almost at once. I still love you, Struan, and I don't
think that's ever going to change. And there's not a
thing I can do about it.'

She never really knew what she'd expected him to say
to that. Did she want him to say he was no longer in
love with Gina, that their marriage had ended anyway,
that there was a way forward for him and Verity? But
she knew that things couldn't be that easy for either of
them—not after all that had happened.

Struan released her. He turned away, his broad
shoulders bowed as if carrying an intolerable burden.
When he spoke again, his voice was heavy.

'No,' he said quietly, 'there isn't. Not a thing.'

CHAPTER SEVEN

IT was a long time before Verity fell asleep that night. As she lay in her lonely bed, aching more than ever before for the feel of Struan's arms about her, her mind returned again and again to the scene in the dining-room. To the agony in Struan's eyes as he'd bitterly accused her of having other men—a bitter jealousy that sprang directly from his tortured uncertainty that she felt anything at all for him. And that had been her fault, she admitted—she'd taken care not to let him know her true feelings, convinced that for him she had never been more than a plaything.

But she could no longer be sure of that—not now that she'd seen the unmistakable pain twisting Struan's face, darkening his eyes. That pain had been as real and as strong as her own, and she had recognised at once that it indicated feelings that were equally deep. But just what feelings were they? Love for herself, a love that had been repressed for five years—or a bitter despair at the break-up of his marriage, a need for physical relief that Verity could provide? She still couldn't be absolutely sure.

Did he love her after all—as perhaps he had always loved her? Or was she no more than a distraction, an escape from his own trapped emotions?

'It would have been better if you'd never come here,' he'd told her down in the dining-room, lines of pain etched sharply on his haunted face. 'Better if you had stayed away. We'd have forgotten—in time we would both have forgotten.'

'You don't believe that,' she whispered, coming close

to him so that their bodies touched. She felt the shudder
go through him and closed her own eyes at the impact.
You could get hurt, she warned herself, hurt even more
badly than the last time. But it made no difference. She
loved Struan, and because he was unhappy she wanted
to give him that love—to do with as he wished. 'You
don't believe it at all. And neither do I.' A sudden surge
of strength caused her to fling her head back proudly,
offering herself for his kiss. 'We both know it isn't true,
Struan. We both know we would never have forgotten.'

For a moment, she thought that he would take her
invitation, bend his lips to hers, take the pliant body she
was offering him. And if he had, she knew with
complete certainty that there would have been no way
of stopping their inevitable lovemaking, no way to
prevent its complete consummation.

There was a moment's breathless silence while she
waited, knowing that Struan was battling with his
desire. *Take me, she wanted to cry, take me and
everything will seem clear* ... But he turned away at
last, leaving her feeling suddenly cold and alone. The
touch of his body on hers, removed now, left an aching
void as if it had been a part of her. Verity shivered and
slowly wrapped her arms round herself. She wondered
desolately if such a moment would ever come again;
and, if it did, whether Struan would act any differently.

Struan was over by the window now, looking out at
the twilit sky. A thin crescent moon was just showing
above the trees that fringed the lawn, and Verity
remembered the saying that it was unlucky to see a new
moon through glass. She stood hesitating in the middle
of the room, wondering if she dared go across to
Struan, wondering what would happen if she did.

But before she could move, Struan had turned and
was facing her, his expression hidden by shadows.

'Verity, we've got to talk,' he said, his voice ragged

with emotion. 'There are things we need to know about
each other—a lot can happen in five years and I . . .'
His voice faltered, then grew stronger. 'There are things
I have to tell you, things you should know. But not
tonight. I need time—time to think. . . .' The deep voice,
its edges roughened like torn velvet, faded again. 'Can
you wait, Verity?' he asked in a husky whisper.

Verity nodded. There was nothing she could say;
until Struan had told her the things that were tearing
him apart, there was nothing she could do but wait. As
he was certain she would, she reflected, for he knew as
well as she did that they were both powerless in the grip
of whatever it was that possessed them.

She'd called it love, she thought as she left him and
climbed slowly up the stairs to her room. But suppose it
were something darker . . .?

Struan had gone before Verity came down next
morning, and she and Lucy ate their breakfast alone at
the kitchen table, not bothering to use the sunny little
breakfast room. Verity felt weary and heavy-eyed,
unable to respond as usual to Lucy's chatter, but she
stirred herself enough to go out and help feed the
rabbits, noting with resignation that Mrs Macgregor
was pregnant again. Honestly, something would have to
be done or they'd be over-run. Struan had told her that
Lucy's crazes never lasted long, but this one was
beginning to get out of hand. She wondered when the
doe would produce her new litter, and found that she
knew less about rabbits than she'd supposed. She would
have to look it up.

Fresh air was what was needed today, she thought,
putting a hand to her muzzy head. A long walk over the
hill. Fortunately Lucy was accustomed to walking—her
father often took her round the estate with him, she said
as they got ready, and she had to walk miles with him

sometimes. He wouldn't mind them going wherever they liked, so long as they didn't hurt the crops. She helped Verity collect together a packed lunch, and they set out.

Spring was giving way now to summer, and the lanes were thick with the foaming wild parsley that Verity had seen before. The hedges were dotted with dog-roses, while the pink flowers of ragged robin and the tall spikes of rosebay willowherb filled the ditches. The fields were full of sturdy lambs, old enough now to leave their mothers for short periods and gather together in mischievous groups, careering around in mad races or jostling to stand on top of a grassy hummock. They stopped their games to stare at Verity and Lucy as they passed, then rushed back to their ewes, thrusting hard little heads underneath for milk, woolly tails wagging ridiculously.

The highlight of the day, for Lucy, was when they were on the way home in the afternoon and came across a family group of wild rabbits, nibbling industriously at a grassy bank which was evidently their home. They fled in panic in all directions, disappearing under bushes and down holes, leaving Lucy thrilled but disappointed. 'I wouldn't have hurt them,' she said sadly, looking at the now deserted bank, 'but of course they didn't know that, did they?'

'We could come back another day and watch them, perhaps,' Verity suggested. 'Creep up so they don't know we're here, and hide behind a bush.' As she said it, she wondered suddenly how long she would be here to do such things with Lucy. It depended on Struan— what it was he wanted her to know about his own situation, whatever that was. Divorced, yes—but there was more to it than that. There was a depth of suffering etched in his face which told Verity that it went deeper than the divorce, back to the marriage itself. Even before that ... And she wondered again why he *had* married Gina, so suddenly and unexpectedly. Was it simply because Lucy was on the way? The result of one mistake, made through loneliness? Had he believed that Verity would be unable to forgive that mistake, or had he decided that his duty now lay with Gina and their unborn child? It sounded possible. Struan was, as Verity had always known, a man of high principles. But surely he could have told her—explained . . .

And even if not, couldn't he tell her now? Couldn't they put the mistake back in the past, where it belonged? Accept Lucy—which would be easy enough, surely—and start afresh.

Or was there some other reason why Struan couldn't shake himself free of the past any more than Verity had been able to?

Struan had said that they needed to talk, but as the days went by it seemed less and less likely that they would. He was gone each morning by the time Verity got up, and came in late each evening, going straight to his office where she had learned not to disturb him. It was like Cox and Box, she thought, and wondered if he were deliberately avoiding her. But it was a busy time on all the estate farms, she knew that, and Struan himself was working in the fields as well as in the office. Lucy had observed that she never saw much of Daddy at this time of year.

'You can't even remember,' Verity had teased her. 'You've only been alive five years, and you can't possibly remember what happened when you were a baby.'

'I can remember a lot,' Lucy informed her with dignity. 'I can remember being in my pram. And I know Daddy's always busy in the summer. Mummy said——' Her face closed suddenly in an almost uncanny imitation of the way Struan's expression

would shut off, and she went back to what she'd been
doing, which was drawing a large and complex picture
of the Macgregor family in the wire netting enclosure
which had been built on the lawn for them. Verity
watched her for a moment, feeling an ache in her heart.
Lucy was so like Struan, it was almost comic, yet it was
somehow sad too that there should be no sign at all that
Gina was her mother. Had Gina ever felt this, searching
her daughter's face for some fleeting resemblance to
herself? Or had she felt—as Verity knew she would have
done—a delight in seeing this small replica of the man
she loved?

And did either of them regret that Lucy hadn't been a
boy, to inherit the estate one day? Had they tried to
have another baby? Was this the key to the breakdown
of their marriage?

To her surprise, Struan came in early that evening
and asked her to eat her dinner with him. When he was
out, Verity had got into the habit of having supper with
Lucy, earlier in the evening, but tonight she took extra
care with the meal, finding something to cook herself
rather than use one of Mrs Weedon's prepared meals. It
was too late to use a frozen chicken, or even the trout
she'd found in the freezer, but she discovered a box full
of ground beef and made a lasagne to go with the fresh
salad that was always coming in from the garden. With
a bowl of early strawberries to follow, she thought the
meal was attractive and tasty, and hoped Struan would
like it too.

Presumably he did—at least, he ate it all and even
asked for more. But that was about all he did say. And
Verity, who hadn't forgotten his promise that they
would talk, found her expectations dying within her.
What was the matter with him? she wondered, looking
at the silent, withdrawn man who sat opposite her. Was
he regretting that scene the other night when she'd

admitted her own feelings and he—well, surely he'd *implied* them? Was he intending to tell her that he didn't want her here any more, that it was best for them all if she left?

I couldn't, she thought with a cold, lonely desperation. I simply couldn't.

They were drinking their coffee in the drawing-room when Struan finally came out of his absorption and spoke to her.

'Verity—I've been thinking.'

She suppressed the reply that she'd guessed he might be, and said merely, 'Oh?' Her heart had begun to thump uncomfortably.

'We need to get away from here for a few hours,' he said, surprising her. 'Isn't Mrs Weedon due home tomorrow?'

'Yes, she is.' And that was the end of their time alone in this house, she thought sadly. Though she didn't really know why it should make any difference, when Lucy had been here all the time. And she hadn't really wanted him to do anything so obvious as come to her room at night, had she? That would have solved nothing.

'So can we have a day out together the next day?' he went on, surprising her again. 'I—I want to see you away from this house, from the farm and the estate. Do you realise, we've only ever known each other here? Apart from that one day when we went to the Farm Park. I think we need to get a different background—to see each other in a different perspective. It might help——' His voice trailed away.

'Help?' Verity said, watching him. The silver glimmer of his eyes was veiled by the dark line of his brows. She saw him lift one hand and run the fingers through his thick black hair.

'Help to sort out what's happening to us,' he said

quietly, and then got up and moved to the window.
'Verity, I know I've been behaving like a coward. We've
got to talk. But—I just have the feeling that, when we
do, everything will change.' He turned and stared across
the room at her. 'I'm afraid,' he said simply, and her
heart went out to him. 'Afraid of what the change
might be. I want one more day with you before I take
the risk—one day in which I can feel secure. If secure is
the word.' A bitterness twisted his features. 'Let's leave
it at—one more day. A day for ourselves and nobody
else, a day out of time. Can we leave Lucy here with
Mrs Weedon the day after tomorrow, then, and have
our own, special day before we go any further?' His
eyes were entreating, dark with the secrets he couldn't
yet bring himself to share.

   There was no way in which Verity could refuse him;
to have done so would have been as painful as refusing
herself. A day out of time. Was it too much to ask?
Especially when she too felt that it might turn out to be
all they were allowed?

Mrs Weedon, refreshed from her holiday, was quite
happy to look after Lucy while she got her kitchen back
in order, and Lucy was temporarily distracted from the
Macgregors by hearing all about Majorca. Neither of
them seemed particularly surprised when Struan
announced that he was taking Verity out for the day.
   The morning was bright and sunny, with just enough
of a breeze to stop it from being humid. Verity tried on
half a dozen different outfits before deciding to wear a
shirtwaister dress in clear blue that caught at her
narrow waist, its open collar flattering her slender neck
and hinting at the shadows between her small, softly-
moulded breasts. The colour of the dress accentuated
the sapphire glow of her eyes and brought out the
golden tan of her skin and the tawny glints in the hair

that curled around her glowing face.

Satisfied at last, she went down and found Struan waiting in the hall, wearing pale fawn, casual slacks and a matching shirt which enhanced the bronzing that had come from working outdoors. He watched her descend the stairs, saying nothing; then, as she reached him, he took her hand.

'Good girl,' he said lightly, 'you didn't keep me waiting. Now we've got the whole day ahead of us, and nobody to please but ourselves.' He led her out to where the car waited, its hood down so that they wouldn't miss any of the sunshine. Verity felt her hand tremble in his, knowing that the lightness of his words was hiding a much deeper emotion. 'No Mrs Weedon, no Lucy,' he went on, opening the door for her. 'No Macgregors—*especially* no Macgregors. Just us.' He went round to the driver's side and slid into his seat, his eyes suddenly intent as he gazed at her. 'It's rather like being given the Crown Jewels to hold for a day.'

Variety's eyes misted and her lips quivered as she smiled at him. She wanted badly at that moment to kiss him—to have those firm lips pressed against hers, to yield completely to whatever demands they might make. If only they had the right to do that, here in full view of anyone who happened to be watching!

But all they had was this one day. And Struan was right. It should be spent as far from Courtneys as possible, far from anyone who might know them, so that just for a few hours they could be carefree and open, living as any other normal couple in love might live.

By now, Verity was sure that this day was all they would ever have. Tonight, she believed, Struan would keep his promise and tell her the true story of his marriage. And she would know that there was nothing left but for her to leave him—this time, for ever.

*　　　*　　　*

There were times that day when they seemed to have
been together for ever, times when Verity felt they'd
only just met. Times when the day seemed to stretch
ahead as if it would never end; times when it rushed
madly towards evening, so that she wanted to catch it in
its flight and make everything stop. Don't go too
quickly, she begged, just slow down a little. But time
ignored her, as time always does.

They spent their day in Bath. It was a city Verity had
never visited, a city where everyone seemed to be on
holiday. The sun shone down on the white streets, on
the graceful curves of Georgian houses, on the towering
abbey that dominated the centre. It glittered on the
wide river with its horseshoe weir, glowed on the
mellow stones of the bridge. The little streets and
squares seemed to belong more to Italy than to
England, which was only reasonable, Verity supposed,
when one remembered the Roman influence. Her hand
in Struan's, she wandered round the old Roman Baths,
trying to picture the men and women who had bathed
here centuries ago. They went to see the hot springs,
tasted the spa water with grimaces, and finally had tea
in the Pump Room to the sound of a musical quartet.

'Have you enjoyed it?' Struan asked, and Verity
nodded, her glowing eyes making the question
unnecessary.

'It's a place I've always wanted to visit. And it's not a
disappointment. It's so elegant—so graceful. It seems
all of a piece—so many cities have been spoiled with
new buildings, and their centres all look the same, with
the same chain stores, the same façades everywhere. But
here—well, even the new buildings fit in without trying
to pretend to be what they're not. The atmosphere is
still intact.'

'Yes, I feel that too.' Struan's eyes were intent, and

Verity knew that he was thinking the same as she was—
that they felt a great many of the same things. That
they had a great deal in common—the emotion that
had always been between them wasn't just a physical
thing. It was a meeting of the minds.

'We're right for each other,' he said quietly, his hand
covering hers on the table. 'Aren't we, Verity?'

Verity nodded. His eyes were drawing her gaze like
twin magnets, like stars. She turned her hand under his,
to grasp it palm to palm, and felt a steady beat that was
more than sexual excitement. 'We belong together,' she
said in a low tone.

'I know. And the hell of it is——' He broke off, his
brows coming together in a frown. 'No, we're not going
to talk about it now. We're going to enjoy today. If we
never have anything else, we'll have this to remember.
What now, Verity? A last walk down by the river and
then dinner somewhere in the country? What would you
like to do most?'

Verity kept her eyes on his, knowing that he wouldn't
mistake even the slightest hint in her meaning.

'I'd like a walk by the river, yes,' she said, tightening
her fingers around his. 'But then—I'd like to go home.
Back to Courtneys. I'd like us to have a quiet dinner
there, together, and then—then you can talk.' And
then, she thought, wondering if her thoughts could
reach him through the charged air between them, or
through the clasp of their hands, if you want to, you
can make love to me. If this is really to be our last day
together, I want that to remember too. I want to know
that for one short day of my life I was entirely,
completely yours.

She was quite sure that Struan understood her. His
eyes darkened in the way that had already become
excitingly familiar, so that her heart kicked and a thin
spiral of desire twisted in her stomach, making her gasp

a little with the force of it. She was even more sure as
they walked by the river, his arm loosely around her
shoulders, her head resting against its warm strength.
And again, as they drove slowly back through the
dreaming lanes, the evening sun warm on their backs.

Tonight, she thought with a fresh leap of desire,
tonight we'll be together whatever Struan has to tell me.
This one night we'll have, whatever tomorrow may
bring. Her heart beat faster as she thought of herself
and Struan, together in her wide bed, free at last of all
inhibitions, able for a few hours to express to the full
everything they felt for each other, all the love and
longing that had been suppressed for the past five years
and had, in the past month, deepened and grown until
it couldn't be held back any longer.

There was a touch of fear in her imaginings too.
Suppose she didn't please him—suppose that in this, the
final proof, she failed him? But it wouldn't happen—it
couldn't. Not when emotion was as powerful as this.

As if Struan sensed her thoughts—or maybe because
he was thinking just the same—he reached out and laid
one hand on her thigh, just above the knee. It was
almost more than she could bear.

'I think,' Struan murmured as he brought the grey
Porsche to a halt outside the house, 'I think we might
just skip dinner tonight, don't you? After all, that was a
fairly substantial lunch we had.'

'I'm not hungry,' Verity murmured, and he slanted a
smile at her that nearly stopped her heart.

'Who said anything about being hungry?' He got out
of the car and held her door open for her. 'You slip in
and tell Mrs Weedon we'll look after ourselves this
evening—she'll be pleased to be able to watch her
favourite TV serial, I'm sure. And I'll go up and make
sure Lucy's asleep. And then——'

But Verity never found out what he was going to say

next. For as they went up the steps together the front door opened. A woman stood there—a thin blonde woman, who looked rather more than five years older, whose chocolate-box prettiness had sharpened into gauntness, whose baby-blue eyes were deep-set and haunted in the pallor of her face.

'So there you are, you two truants!' The voice was as fluting as ever, though wasn't its tone just very slightly cracked now, as if it were tangibly brittle and could break at any moment? 'Lucy and I almost got tired of waiting—in fact, she went to bed half an hour ago.' The woman came forward, holding out her hands, a smile of almost grotesque gaiety on her face. 'So you're Verity—Lucy's nanny. And such a beautiful nanny, too. Has Struan told you you're beautiful? Well, I'm sure if he hasn't, other men have. And Struan—aren't you going to welcome your wife home?'

'Hello, Gina.' Struan moved forward, and as Verity watched, feeling as if she'd been frozen to the spot, he took Gina by her shoulders and kissed her gently. 'This is quite a surprise. Do you intend to stay for long?'

'Well, of course I do, Struan.' The laughter was as brittle as the voice. 'I've come home for ever. To stay. This *is* my home, after all—isn't it?'

CHAPTER EIGHT

'YOU won't want me in your way,' Verity said after what seemed a lifetime, her voice sounding as if it came from a long way off. 'I'll have my meal in the kitchen with Mrs Weedon. It—it's nice to meet you, Mrs ...' Mrs Courtney—was that what Gina called herself now? Verity didn't know, and in any case her tongue refused to utter the name and her voice trailed away.

Anyway, it wasn't true. Seeing Gina was a shock she was entirely unprepared for, and even if she'd been expecting it there would have been little pleasure in the meeting. What was even worse was Gina's appearance—it might have helped in some obscure way if she'd still been the pretty, chocolate-box girl Verity had seen just before the wedding. But those thin cheeks, those hollow eyes, the almost ugly boniness of a body that had once been prettily curved—all this could only have been caused by suffering. Verity felt suddenly ashamed. This woman had been Struan's wife, the victim of a trauma that had obviously affected her as deeply as him, and only a few moments ago Verity had been planning to go to bed with him, thinking that the act of making love could wipe out his torment. Now, looking at Gina's ravaged face, she knew that it couldn't, that it had been a shallow hope. She wondered how Struan was feeling at this moment, but didn't dare look at him.

'Have your meal in the *kitchen*?' Gina echoed. 'But you can't do that—you're a friend of the family, or so Lucy would have me believe. Didn't you know Struan years ago? And you've been out for the day with him now—he wouldn't want to relegate you to the kitchen.

130

Would you, my sweet?' She turned her face up to Struan's, and Verity wondered just what Gina Courtney wanted. Was she hoping to get her husband back, to persuade him to remarry her? Or was she simply reminding Verity that Struan had been *her* husband— that, even as his ex-wife, she still retained certain rights and priorities? 'Of course you'll eat with us,' Gina went on quickly. 'You're not a *servant*.'

'Well, I am in a way—I'm Lucy's nanny, after all. Struan was going to engage a Miss Morris, but she broke her leg on the way here for an interview, and as I was already here——' She was talking too much, but the abrupt transition from being Struan's acknowledged lover—and that's what she had almost been, surely?— to a 'friend of the family' was proving too much for her. She wanted nothing so much as to get away. 'I'd like to join you for dinner, if you're really sure,' she went on, gathering together all the poise she'd acquired in the past five years. 'I'll just slip upstairs first and see that Lucy's all right, and then I'll change. Dinner won't be ready for a while, will it?'

'No, Mrs Weedon's busy with fatted calves at this minute.' Gina gave her another friendly smile before linking her arm with Struan's. 'Do you want to change too, darling? Shall I come with you and talk while you do? Or shall we just have a cosy drink together in the drawing-room?'

Verity made for the stairs, giving Struan a glance as she reached them. To her surprise, he was standing quite still, staring down at Gina's upturned face with an odd expression that was half-exasperation, half-despair. One hand was still resting on his wife's shoulder, and as Verity watched she saw the fingers tighten, as if he were suffering some extreme emotion.

Could it be love? she wondered as she turned quickly away and went on up. A realisation that it had been

Gina all along, that Verity had just happened to arrive at the psychological moment when he needed a woman? Was he feeling an even deeper shame than Verity at what had so nearly happened?

If so, it wouldn't be long before Verity knew for certain. In her state of hypersensitivity to Struan's emotions, she couldn't help but know if it were Gina whom Struan loved. And if it were . . .

There would be no place then for Verity Sandison at Courtney Grange.

Dinner that night was the most uncomfortable meal Verity had ever experienced.

She dressed carefully for it, not wanting Gina to have any suspicion that Struan might be more interested in her than he might be in any nanny. Wondering just what explanation he'd given for having taken her out for the day, she chose a plain, dark blue skirt and white blouse with tiny tucks in the front. Her hair was just long enough to catch up in a pleat above her slim neck, the shorter curls at the front escaping to form a wispy aureole round her small face. She looked in the mirror when she was ready, satisfied with her appearance as a rather staid, even old-fashioned nanny. She had no idea that the restraint she'd tried to suggest hinted instead at a hidden, smouldering sensuality, nor that the burning darkness of her eyes completed the illusion.

Downstairs, she saw that Struan and Gina had both changed, and wondered immediately if they had done so together, wandering in and out of the bedroom with its adjoining bathroom half-dressed and chatting companionably. Or maybe even more—it wasn't impossible, was it, that in the intervening hour they'd found time to make love? Gina had certainly come here for some reason, after all, and Struan at least had been in a highly-charged emotional state—wouldn't it have been perfectly natural for him to relieve his sexual feelings with his ex-wife? It was, after all, probably her absence that had caused them.

Stop torturing yourself, she thought as Struan handed her a drink. He didn't have to ask her what she wanted—Martini and lemonade, cool and refreshing, was what she always asked for. He had the same, but filled Gina's glass with orange juice before going to stand in his favourite place by the window.

'So tell me all about yourself,' Gina invited, coming to sit beside Verity on the couch. 'Didn't you have a famous sister—a model, wasn't she? Let me see——' She clicked her thin fingers. 'Sophie, wasn't that her name? What's she doing now, is she still modelling?'

'No, she's married now.' So much for Gina's first question, Verity thought wryly, but she fastened thankfully on to the subject of Sophie. 'She married a rather nice Texan—Robert Redford to the life—and they live in New York.' She risked a glance at Struan, but he was standing by the window, looking remote and unapproachable. 'I don't see a lot of them, of course, but I've been over once to stay and Sophie comes to London occasionally. They keep asking me to go over for longer—live there for a while.'

'But that would be wonderful! Why don't you? You'd find a job easily, I'm sure—English nannies are at a premium there, aren't they?'

Verity blinked. She had almost forgotten that she was supposed to be a nanny—when Sophie and Ed had suggested she might go, it was as a writer they'd been thinking of. Ed knew quite a few magazine editors in New York, and was sure there'd be an opening for someone from England—someone go-ahead like Verity, able to tackle difficult subjects as well as profiles on celebrities. Once or twice, wondering how to free herself from the shackles of her past, she'd even half-

considered it. But she'd never quite been able to say yes;
perhaps because she'd never been able to contemplate
leaving the country where Struan Courtney still lived.

They went in to dinner, and the talk was more
general, though as the meal progressed Gina's
conversation became more and more centred on herself.
She asked Verity questions about London, following
them immediately with stories of her own about shows
she'd seen there, nightclubs she'd visited, friends and
parties. Verity began to get a picture of a restless,
disjointed life spent in a fruitless search for something
that, like a will o' the wisp, always managed to evade
her.

As they began the main course, a shoulder of lamb
with fresh peas and new potatoes, Gina looked round
the table.

'No wine?' she exclaimed. 'Struan, you surely don't
intend to celebrate my homecoming in mineral water?'

'I'm quite happy to do so,' he returned evenly. 'I
know alcohol doesn't suit you at present.'

'Oh, but you and Verity must have something.' Gina
jumped up and went to the door, but Struan was there
before her. 'Don't be silly, Struan—I'm sure you
usually have a bottle of wine.'

'Indeed we don't, not every evening.' His voice was
firm. 'It doesn't matter, Gina. I'm sure Verity doesn't
mind. There's nothing suitable chilled this evening—if
I'd known you were coming, naturally I'd have had
champagne—but as it is we'll make do with this very
pleasant and healthy spring water.'

'*Don't* you mind, Verity?' Gina asked with an
incredulous note to her voice. 'I can't drink myself, as
Struan's said—these wretched tablets I have to take—
but I hate to sit there and know that you're not having
any either.'

'I don't mind at all.' It was quite true that they rarely

did drink wine with their evening meal, Struan being an abstemious man who preferred to keep alcohol for celebrations—but didn't this count as one? Though if Gina didn't drink ... And perhaps it didn't. Perhaps that closed expression concealed a frustration which was as bitter as her own.

Gina came back to the table and sat down, shrugging a little. 'Well, if you're sure. But tomorrow we'll celebrate properly—I might even have a tiny one myself, in spite of what the doctors say——' She raised her eyes in a gesture of defiance at Struan, who gave her a brief glance and said curtly, 'I don't think you will, Gina. You want to get better, don't you?'

Gina picked up her knife and fork, looking as mutinous as Lucy did when she was balked. So there was some resemblance after all, Verity thought, seeing the pushed-out underlip and sulky eyes. Perhaps Lucy had inherited her occasional flashes of temper from her mother too.

The rest of the meal passed without incident, and directly afterwards Verity excused herself and went up to her room. She closed the door behind her and leaned on it, letting out a sigh of relief. Being with Gina and Struan was like walking a tightrope, she thought. It was difficult to see how she could continue without falling.

Gina stayed in bed until nearly lunchtime next day, and then came down only to lie on a long chair in the garden with a pile of glossy magazines. She demanded Lucy's company for a while, but soon grew bored with the conversation, which was as usual mainly about rabbits, and showed no enthusiasm for a visit to the Macgregors. After about half an hour, she lay back, closed her eyes, and told Lucy that she was tired.

'I have to sleep a lot, I'm afraid, darling,' she said. 'You go with Verity and do something energetic, and

I'll see you again at teatime. It'll be a good thing when she goes to school in September,' she added to Verity. 'She needs something to occupy her mind. All this interest in rabbits, it doesn't seem healthy.'

'Oh, it's just a phase,' Verity said. 'Though she does seem interested in all animals, especially wildlife. It's something to be encouraged, I think. And only natural, when she lives in the country. I suppose she takes after her father.'

Gina opened her eyes and gave Verity an odd look. She seemed to be considering something, but she only said, 'Yes. I expect so,' and closed her eyes again. She really did look exhausted, Verity thought, looking down at her, and she wondered whether Gina had really been fit to come home yet.

She wondered again when she next saw her, a couple of hours later when she and Lucy had come back for tea. Gina was sitting up now, the tray on a low table beside her, and she was looking flushed and bright-eyed. Better, Verity thought at first with some surprise, but then she began to wonder. Wasn't Gina's sudden vivacity somewhat unnatural? Almost feverish? She wondered what had happened while she and Lucy had been away exploring the woods—perhaps someone had called. But if they had, Gina didn't mention it. She poured tea and offered cakes as brightly as if she were a society hostess holding a garden party, laughing and talking so animatedly that Verity and Lucy had to join in.

'I'll put Lucy to bed and read to her tonight,' Gina announced later as they sat on the lawn. 'Yes, I'm quite all right, and I ought to be doing my motherly duties. You sit here and rest for a while. I know how exhausting my daughter can be. Don't worry about a thing until dinner, and that's an order!'

Verity lay back in her chair. There was something in

this abrupt change in Gina that made her feel uneasy, but she couldn't pin down what it was. The contrast between Gina's earlier indifference and the interest that now seemed rather forced—or was that being catty? Gina had been ill, still wasn't fully recovered, that was obvious to anyone. She'd probably been feeling weak and tired after lunch, needing a rest. Now that she'd had it, she felt better. Maybe any medication she had to take had helped.

Verity faced the fact that she herself might be jealous of Gina, jealous of the fact that she was Lucy's mother and therefore entitled to her affection. She moved her head restlessly against the back of her chair and groaned aloud.

Wasn't it enough to be jealous of Gina's relationship with Struan? Wasn't it enough that she'd spent almost the whole of last night awake, unable to stop herself imagining them together, unable to prevent the pictures in her mind of Gina's fragile body cradled in Struan's arms, of the lovemaking that he would make as gentle as possible, the tenderness of his kisses and caresses? Verity had made every effort to stop her thoughts, reading book after book in a futile attempt to distract herself. But nothing had worked. The print had danced before her eyes in a spiteful mockery of her attempts, and she had ended up sitting by the window and staring out at the dawn, her eyes sore with the misery of tears she refused to shed, her heart aching with the love she couldn't express.

Why had Gina come back? she wondered for the hundredth time. What was there here that she couldn't let go? Was it Lucy, her daughter? Or was it the husband she had parted from, ostensibly for ever?

And if it was Gina's plan to persuade Struan into remarriage, what were his feelings? He had given no sign of asking her to leave. Did that mean that he, too, regretted the divorce?

And if so—where did that leave Verity?

At dinner, however, Verity found that she and Struan had other problems on their hands.

Gina had not yet come downstairs when Verity arrived in the drawing-room, and she hesitated in the doorway, reluctant to go in. Struan was over by the window, pouring drinks, his back to the door, and she was able to stand for a moment observing him. He looked tired, she thought, and then—well, there was probably a very good reason for that. And her imaginings of the night before came flooding back.

'Martini and lemonade?' Struan asked, turning suddenly, and Verity felt her colour deepen. She hadn't realised he'd heard her come in. But perhaps he hadn't needed to. As she came over to take her drink, she was aware of the current between them, as highly-charged and potent as it had ever been. Either of them would, she knew, be aware that the other was in the same room without having to look.

His eyes were on hers with that dark, intent look which made her heart twist. Was he trying to tell her something, trying to give her some message—that nothing had changed between them, that it was all as it had been before Gina came back? But how can it be? she wanted to cry. She was your *wife*. You spent last night with her—didn't you?—making love. How can you tell me that nothing has altered?

Straun's expression changed and he took a step towards her. If he touches me, I won't be able to bear it, she thought, and her breath caught in her throat. Struan, touch me, touch me, she implored with her eyes.

The door opened, and Struan stepped away. Verity clung to her glass, not daring to look round, too confused to know whether she was relieved or not.

'Oh, there you are!' Gina sounded brittle and gay, as if she'd been searching for them in some game of hide-and-seek. 'And you've started drinks already, without waiting for me. Pour me something strong, Struan darling, will you? I feel I need it after putting that child to bed. God, she's exhausting.' She came further into the room and Verity looked at her, shocked by the high colour in Gina's cheeks, the unnatural glitter in her eyes. 'You have my deep admiration, Verity.' She seemed to have slight difficulty with the word 'admiration'.

'Gina, what have you been doing?' Struan asked sternly. He didn't attempt to pour her a drink, and Verity had a sudden flash of premonition. She watched as the other girl crossed the room, swaying slightly.

'Doing? Simply putting our daughter to bed, what's wrong with that?' Gina reached the drinks table and put out her hand for the bottle of gin, but Struan was there first and caught her wrist in a powerful grasp. 'Struan, let go—you're hurting me! Can't I have a little drink, now I've carried out my duty as a mother? You and Verity both are.'

'You've already had a drink, and not such a little one, either,' Struan said grimly. 'Gina, don't be a fool. You know what it will do to you. Now, tell me—how much have you had?'

'Not much. Not enough.' Gina flung back her head and stared at him with a mixture of defiance and— Verity saw with a shock—abject misery. 'You can't tell me what to do and what not to do any more,' she told him, enunciating her words with care. 'I'm not your wife now. And you can't tell me to go away, either, much as you'd like to—oh yes, I know what you'd like

to do, you can't fool me. You want me to go away so
that you can carry on with *her*.' She flung out a white
arm, pointing with a trembling finger at Verity. 'A
nanny—your child's nanny. But she's my child too and
I've a right to come and see her whenever I like. And I
shall. And if I want to stay with her, I'll stay, and
there's not a damned thing you can do to stop me!' Her
face crumpled suddenly. Verity cast a desperate glance
at Struan. What should she do—what did he want her
to do? Stay here and help—or leave him and Gina to
their own private agonies?

But Struan was staring at Gina, his expression a
mixture of pity, exasperation and sombre despair. With
a sudden insight, Verity realised that Gina was drunk,
had been drunk before she even came into the room.
Drunk while she put her daughter to bed ... Lucy!
Verity made a quick move towards the door. She must
go and see that the child was all right.

'Don't go, Verity!' It was almost a wail, and stopped
Verity in her tracks. 'Don't leave me alone with Struan.
He's cross with me, and I hate it when he's cross with
me. That's the trouble, you see—he's *always* been cross
with me. Ever since we were married. It was never a
proper marriage—I knew it couldn't be. And I was
right. It was a punishment, and it's gone on being a
punishment ever since.' The once-pretty face was ugly
and grotesque now, distorted with tears, the mouth
working piteously. 'Tell him it wasn't my fault, Verity.
Tell him I couldn't help it—any of it. I didn't know
what to do—where to turn. And when he said he'd
marry me—well, what would *you* have done?'

She collapsed into a chair, her head buried in her
arms, weeping noisily and uncontrollably. Verity stared
at her, then at Struan. She felt helpless and inadequate,
unable to cope. What Gina had said made no sense,
though she had an idea it might later on, when she had

time to think about it. But there wasn't time now. Gina
needed help—and so did Struan.

He was standing quite still staring down at the thin,
shaking shoulders of his ex-wife. For a few moments he
made no effort to touch her or offer any comfort. The
look on his face was as tightly controlled as Verity had
ever seen it, but she knew that in his mind he was
feeling both pity and disgust. Whether love was there
also she couldn't tell.

'What had we better do?' she asked in a low voice.
'Get her to bed?'

He nodded. 'It's the only thing. Will you help me? I
could carry her, but I'm afraid she'll struggle and
perhaps hurt herself. Once she's there, she'll probably
sleep.'

Between them, they helped Gina to her feet. She hung
between them like a rag doll, weeping more quietly
now, the tears running down her face in a cascade. Her
flash of energy seemed to have dissipated itself, and she
made no demur when they led her gently to the door
and up the stairs.

'In here.' Struan indicated the room at the end of the
landing. So he and Gina hadn't shared a room last
night—or had they? The fact that he was taking her in
here now, opening the door that led to the big, sunny
room with its wide double bed, proved nothing.

'Here. Lay her down.' They swung Gina's feet on
to the bed and Verity straightened up, looking down
at the frail figure. She had never expected to see
Struan's ex-wife in these circumstances ... 'Do you
want any help in getting her to bed?' she asked, her
throat dry.

'No, I can manage, thanks.' Well, of course he could!
'You go downstairs, Verity—have a drink.' His mouth
twisted wryly as he realised what he had said. 'I'll be
down as soon as she's settled.' He raised his eyes for a

moment and gave Verity a brief, disturbing glance. 'You will be there, won't you? You won't go away?'

There was a current of urgency in his voice, and Verity responded to it as he must have known she would. She shook her head, feeling a slight warming of her chilled body.

'I won't go away,' she promised, and left the room.

Struan would have to talk to her now, she thought as she went down the stairs after checking that Lucy was safely asleep. He couldn't put it off any longer. And then, she would have to make her own decision as to what came next.

One thing was certain. Both Struan and Gina were too vulnerable to be hurt any more. Whatever problems had caused this appalling breakdown, Verity certainly couldn't add to them.

But what had Gina meant when she'd said that Struan had been angry with her ever since their marriage? Was Verity more involved, in fact, than she'd realised? Was it possible that Gina had known about her—known about the tender romance which had blossomed in the fields and woods around Courtneys, known that even as they stood together at the altar Struan's heart had been with another girl? The next second she knew it couldn't be that. Gina had referred to a punishment—a punishment to herself, as if she too bore a burden of guilt for a marriage that had been wrong from the start. So just what could have been so badly, so terribly wrong? Verity stood in the drawing-room, staring out at the sunlit garden, and shivered. The room seemed suddenly icily cold. And you think *you've* been suffering for the past five years, she thought savagely. Why, it's nothing to what's been happening here at Courtneys.

It seemed a long time before Struan came down. Mrs

Weedon looked in to see if they were ready for dinner, and Verity had to tell her that Mrs Courtney had been taken ill, wondering if the housekeeper knew what was the matter. Possibly she did—there might well have been scenes like this before the divorce. From Struan's grim acceptance of the situation, it seemed likely that this wasn't the first time he'd had to carry Gina up the stairs and put her to bed. But why? Was her drinking the cause of their break-up—or was it the other way round?

At last the door opened again and Struan came in.

He looked ten years older, Verity thought, with sudden compassion as he sat down heavily in a chair, and she took a step forward, wanting to go and offer comfort, let him rest his head against her breast. But she stopped—would he want her now? Would he want anyone, or would he rather be alone, to nurse his wounds in private?

Struan answered the question by lifting one hand, and Verity put her own into it, returning the sudden desperate clasp with a gentle squeeze. She moved closer and he leaned his head against her body. Verity touched his head with her free hand, moved the fingers tenderly through the thick hair, and she felt him sigh.

'I suppose Mrs Weedon wants to serve dinner,' he said at last, his voice dry with weariness. 'It must be spoiled by now.'

'It's all right. She's put it all in the trolley to keep hot, we can serve it ourselves. Do you want it now?'

'We might as well. We have to eat, after all, and there's no sense in hurting her feelings.' Struan lifted himself from his chair and walked slowly across to the dining-room door. 'And then we'll talk.' He glanced at Verity with a look that was almost fearful. 'That's if you still want to, if you don't want to pack your bags and get out before you're contaminated too.'

'Of course I want to. We have to.' Verity kept her voice firm. 'And I've no intention of packing my bags—not until you tell me to, anyway.'

Struan said nothing to that. He sat down at the table while Verity took the hot dishes from the heated trolley and helped him to meat and vegetables. She put rather less on her own plate, feeling sure she wouldn't be able to eat a thing, but to her surprise found that she was hungry after all. And the food made her feel better—not happier, but stronger, more able to cope. The cheesecake was beyond her, however, and she was glad when they were back in the drawing-room with their coffee.

'Well, and now we'd better talk, hadn't we?' Struan said. His face was lit by the tawny glow of sunset, but in spite of the rich, vibrant colours it looked sombre and dark. 'In the first place, I want to make one thing quite clear. Gina is *not* an alcoholic—although I couldn't blame you if you thought she was. But she is ill—has been for a long time.' He sighed, running his fingers through his hair. 'I'm still not really sure whether her illness is physical or not. They say it isn't, though it exhibits quite a lot of physical symptoms. But mostly they call it depression—a particular kind of depression. I don't know if you know anything at all about that kind of thing?'

'Yes, I do,' Verity said soberly. 'I know a bit about depression.' She had written an article about it for one of the leading women's magazines, an exploration of how it affected women in particular and which women were most at risk. But this wasn't the time to tell Struan that.

'That saves me from a lot of explanation, then,' Struan said. 'But to understand Gina's particular problem, you need to know quite a lot about our marriage.' He paused, then added, 'Everything, in fact.'

'Struan, I don't——'

'You don't want to intrude?' he interrupted bitterly, reading her mind with an accuracy that reminded her she couldn't hide anything from this man. 'Is that what you were about to say? It's too late for that, Verity, isn't it? You have intruded. And in fact—it always was too late. You were involved right from the start.'

'So it's all my fault,' Verity said hopelessly. 'Oh God, if only I hadn't come to Lane End in the first place. If only Dad and I had chosen some other village to live.'

'It wouldn't have made any difference,' he told her quietly. 'Oh, I might never have met you, might never have known that somewhere in the world there was a woman who was just right for me, who was meant for me. I might have gone right through life never knowing what I was missing. But it wouldn't have made any difference between Gina and me. Because we were never in love, you see. It wasn't ever a real marriage, and never could have been.' He turned away, running his hand restlessly through his hair, staring blindly out of the window at a sky that seemed to be on fire. 'But since we *did* meet—and since you've come back into my life—we can't try to pretend it never happened. I have to tell you everything, Verity.' He turned back, and his eyes were haunted as he stared at her, their glimmer reflecting the flames of the sky so that they looked like twin torches burning in his face. 'You have to know— you have to let me share it with you, or I don't think I can go on.'

'So tell me,' Verity said quietly, and she came over and sank down on the floor at his feet, leaning against his knees and looking up at his face. 'Tell me what's happened to you, and what it's all about.'

What Struan said next would set the tone for the rest of their lives. It was a crisis, and one that they both recognised. But it had to be faced—faced and accepted. From this moment, there was no escape.

CHAPTER NINE

STRUAN was silent for a few minutes before he began to speak, and Verity sat quietly waiting, leaning against the warm strength of his knees. This wasn't, she knew, a moment to be hurried. Struan was going to tell her things that he had perhaps never told anyone else, things that had remained locked in his heart for years. They would have to be told slowly, with care, and probably also with pain.

'It was only a few weeks before our marriage that I met Gina,' Struan began, his voice low and faraway as if he were talking about another world. 'While you were away in Portugal. She was different then. Pretty in an old-fashioned sort of way, with permed hair and dresses that showed off her figure—you know, plunging necklines and tight waists. A man's woman, someone once called her, all blatant sex-appeal.'

'And she appealed to you?' Verity prompted as he fell silent, though the idea of such obvious charms appealing to Struan's fastidious taste was strange to her.

'Not especially. Oh, I got the message all right—no man could have failed to do that. But for me she would have been no more than a one-night stand, and I've never gone in for that kind of thing.' He hesitated, and then said, 'I have had two other relationships that got quite serious, but neither of them worked completely. There was always something missing, something that I knew I'd find in a woman if I waited long enough.' His eyes came down to her face, dark and tormented. 'And I was right, wasn't I? I'd already found it in you—and,

146

as I'd always known I would, I recognised it the moment I saw you. Walking across that meadow on a sunny morning, your basket over your arm, looking for all the world like someone in a fairy-tale—my own, personal fairy-tale. It was totally unexpected—and, at that moment, a shock.'

'Go back to what you were saying about Gina,' Verity said softly.

'Yes. Well, the first day I saw Gina we were in the churchyard. It was a cold day—cold and bright and windy. There were snowdrops under some yew trees in the corner, and little spots of yellow and purple—the colour of spring flowers—on the graves. The grave we were standing by was freshly-dug and it was covered with wreaths—exotic bouquets of lilies and suchlike—that looked all wrong. It was——' He paused and, suddenly cold with premonition, Verity filled in the gap.

'Your brother's grave? Justin's?'

'Yes, that's right.' Struan's face was brooding, his eyes fixed on the window. The fiery colours of the sky were fading now to a gentler rose, the trees at the edge of the lawn dark silhouettes. 'Well, you can probably guess how the rest of the story goes. Gina was Justin's fiancée. Whether it would have lasted, whether he would really have married her nobody can know. But she was wearing his ring and she was obviously genuinely in love with him. There wasn't any sexual invitation in her manner that day, when we met beside the grave. She was just a heartbroken girl, and she was alone. I couldn't leave her like that.'

'Did—did you ever think you might be in love with her?' Verity asked tentatively, and his head came round with a snap.

'In love with Gina? Never! It wasn't like that at all, Verity. It was much more complicated—although it seemed simple enough at the time. You see, there wasn't only Gina to consider, as I discovered when I took her out to dinner that night—to reassure her that she wasn't entirely alone,' he added ironically. 'You see, she and Justin had been lovers. And she was pregnant.'

'*Lucy*!' Verity breathed, staring at him.

'Yes. Lucy. Justin's child. Possibly—for all we knew—Justin's son. The child who would, if Justin had lived and had married Gina as presumably he intended to, have been Justin's heir.' There was another silence, and this time Verity didn't try to prompt him. She waited, her mind whirling, and after a while Struan said, his voice dry with urgency, 'Do you see now why I had to marry her? In other circumstances, I could have helped her financially and left it at that. There's little stigma in being a single-parent family these days, especially when the father has died ... But this child had rights of its own. Money wasn't enough. If it had turned out to be a boy it would have been the rightful heir to the estate, the estate *I'd* inherited through Justin's death. I had to redress the situation, and the only way I could do it was to marry Gina and accept the child as my own. Then, later, he would inherit from me as he should have done from Justin.'

Verity sat quite still, trying to assimilate these new ideas. She thought of Lucy, who bore such a strong resemblance to Struan that nobody would have questioned the fact that he was her father. But the resemblance was to Justin as well—Verity had seen a portrait of him amongst the others on the walls of the dining-room, and his dark good looks, though glossier than Struan's, were clearly of the family stamp.

'You behave exactly as if Lucy's your daughter,' she said wonderingly. 'Nobody would ever realise——'

Struan made an impatient gesture. 'Well, of course I do. I made up my mind from the beginning that I had to do that. And it hasn't been difficult. You know

Lucy. She's got all the Courtney charm, the charm my brother had, plus a practical streak that I find very endearing. She's the daughter I would have chosen anyway.'

'But she *is* a daughter. Didn't you feel——'

'That I needn't have done it?' His mouth moved in a small twist of bitterness. 'I had other reasons for thinking that by the time Lucy was born ... But no, not simply because she turned out to be a girl after all. The girls of this family are provided for, too, with a trust fund, so Lucy still has an inheritance. The estate itself goes to another part of the family ... if I have no son of my own ...'

The next question was too painful to ask. Had Struan and Gina ever tried to have a son? Had they ever lain together in that big bed, making love in the hope that it might result in an heir for Courtneys? Verity shivered. Put like that, it sounded so cold and calculating. You couldn't call it making love. Love never came into it.

'It's all very feudal, isn't it?' Struan said, interrupting her painful thoughts. 'Our ancestors had quite a lot to answer for in the way they arranged these things.'

'Oh, Struan, I'm so sorry,' Verity said impulsively, reaching her hands up to draw him down to her. 'It was all so well-meant, and it all went wrong. And just because I——'

'No,' he said, 'not just because you came to live at Lane End. Not just because I was already in love with you. Oh, that didn't help, I admit. It turned a mistake into a disaster. And seeing you there that morning just before the wedding, I was filled with a sudden rage against fate for doing this to me—to us. It seemed like a deliberate act of cruelty, and I couldn't even say the things I had to say to you, not properly. And the things I *wanted* to say had to remain in my heart. I couldn't tell you, Verity. I knew that if I did—I wouldn't be able

to go through with it. I'd have to call the whole thing
off, abandon Gina and her child—Justin's child. And
that was something I would never be able to live with.
So I had to be cruel—I had to hurt you enough to make
you never want to see me again. You'll never know just
how hard that was, how painful for me as well as for
you. It's haunted me ever since.' His hand moved
convulsively over her hair. 'When you came back a few
weeks ago, I didn't know if I could bear to have you
near me—and then I knew I couldn't bear not to. I
wanted you so much, Verity, yet I dared not ask you to
share my life. I couldn't even trust myself by then, and
it didn't seem possible that you would be able to trust
me. I'd already let you down once—how could either of
us be sure I'd never do it again? How could I ask you to
take the risk?'

Verity closed her eyes, her whole being concentrating
on the feel of Struan's hand in her hair, tangling with
the red-gold curls that tonight she had left loose,
stroking her neck with a gentleness that failed to hide
the tension in his fingers, the tension that ran through
her body like an electric shock. She turned and laid her
lips on his palm, and he reached for her own hand and
lifted it to his face.

'It could never have worked for Gina and me,' he
went on quietly. 'We both knew that our marriage had
been a mistake. We knew it from the beginning, I
suppose, although we tried for a while to pretend. But
Gina couldn't accept me as a husband—she was still in
love with Justin, still grieving for him. And I couldn't
force myself on her, even if I'd wanted to. There was
nobody in the world I wanted then but you. The
thought of making love to Gina's body, already
occupied by Justin's child—I simply couldn't have done
it.'

'And after the baby—after Lucy was born?'

'Gina never really recovered,' he said soberly. 'It was a difficult birth and she was weak for a long time afterwards. At first, she rejected the baby completely— then she wanted her with a kind of hunger that was almost frightening. She was suffering from post-natal depression, the doctors said, and I knew that she was still grieving for Justin. She actually felt she'd betrayed him by marrying me, and I knew that she would have been happier if I had done what I first considered and simply given her financial help. I believe she could have coped then, with her grief and with the baby. As it was——' He shrugged. 'Our marriage made it impossible for her.' His face was sombre as he stared at the now-darkening sky. 'She had a period when she seemed to go wild, trying to forget—going to London, taking up with the friends she'd known when she was with Justin, going to endless parties and nightclubs. But that didn't help, and eventually she began to drink, just a little at first, and then more and more. She broke down entirely one terrible night, and we both knew that the end had come. Divorce was the only answer for both of us—the only way to save her sanity. But even that, carried out with the least bitterness possible—after all, neither of us was really at fault, except for trying to go against the laws of nature, of love—even then, it was a trauma, and she's needed treatment ever since. Her doctors say that she'll recover in time, but meanwhile she can't cope without drugs. And the ones she takes mean that she mustn't take any alcohol—it intensifies the effects.' His mouth twisted wryly. 'I doubt if she'd had more than a sherry when she came downstairs this evening. As for why she had it—well, I suppose coming back was just too much for her to cope with.'

'But why did she come back?' Verity asked, and he shrugged.

'It was part of our agreement. Although she'd

rejected Lucy, and agreed that she should stay here, the doctors warned me that to refuse access could tip her right over the edge. And she *is* Lucy's mother, and loves her, although she could never take on the responsibility of looking after her. So I promised that she could come back to see Lucy whenever she liked—it was no use trying to tie her down to set times.' He paused, and added quietly, 'I also promised that if she wanted to, she could stay. And now——' his fingers tightened in her hair '—now you know why I could never tell you I loved you—never ask you to share my life. How could I, when at any time Gina might walk back into it?' His eyes caught Verity's, burning with naked hunger. 'Is this to be the pattern of my life, Verity? Tied to a woman who feels nothing for me, who never stops mourning my own brother, yet who wouldn't be able to live without me? Because there must be something here she needs, something she comes back for. And whatever it is, I can't take it away from her. I've helped to ruin her life, and I can't abandon her now, any more than I could five years ago.'

He dropped his head into his hands, and Verity caught him to her with a soft sound of protest. Protest against the circumstances which had brought him this torment, which had tangled him and Gina and Verity herself in a knot that could never be untied. And Lucy, too, she reminded herself. Lucy was bound up in it as well, and was sure to be more and more affected by it as she grew older.

'God, what a mess,' Struan whispered against her hair. 'Verity, what's the answer? What am I to do?'

There was nothing she could say, but the closeness of Struan's body in her arms was answer enough. Verity tightened her clasp and felt him respond. His heartbeat was strong against her breast, and she could feel the race of her own, a rapid fluttering like the wings of a caged bird desperate to escape. Her breath came more quickly, but as yet there was no sexual excitement in the kisses she scattered through his thick, tousled hair, only an overpowering desire to give him the only comfort she knew. She felt the groan shudder through him, felt the change in his body as he shifted his position so that it was now he who held her. And now it was his mouth that was seeking hers, his head moving blindly as she continued to kiss his face and neck, driven by a need she barely understood. He trailed his mouth across her face, moving it against her ears and neck before finding what he sought. Their lips met at last; a sigh that was almost relief swept through them both as they relaxed against each other; and then it was beginning again, a wild, surging excitement that drove them both on and would take no denial. The point of no return, Verity thought dazedly, and knew that they had passed it and this time there must be no holding back. Whatever happened after this, Struan's need—and her own—had to come first. It had been inevitable from the very first time they had met, in that flower-filled meadow, that this would have to happen in the end. It could not be held off any longer.

Slowly, she drew away from Struan, shaking her head at his muttered protests. 'I'm not running away,' she whispered. 'I just want us both to be more comfortable—I don't want any risk of interruption. Can—can we go upstairs?'

His eyes were clearing now, staring at her with a dawning incredulity, and she nodded.

'I want it as much as you do,' she said softly, 'but I don't want anything to go wrong. It may——' her voice shook '—it may be our only time. Come up to my room, Struan, and love me.'

Slowly, he got to his feet, taking her hand, and they left the drawing-room together and went up the stairs as if in a dream. At the top of the stairs they hesitated, both aware of Gina behind one of the closed doors; and then they turned away and went into the room that Verity had occupied ever since she'd come to Courtneys.

Struan closed the door and took her in his arms.

'Verity, my darling.' His voice was husky. 'Are—are you sure you want this? You won't regret it?'

'I want it and I won't regret it,' she said steadily, and he caught her against him with a groan. At the impact of their bodies, a burning excitement flared up in Verity, a desire that this time nothing could stop. She clung to him, winding her legs about his body as he lifted her and carried her to the bed. Gently, he laid her down and looked at her, and then he was bending to undo the buttons of her dress, his fingers trembling so that she had to help him. He pushed aside the thin material and stared at her breasts, swelling against their lacy prison, and he slid his hands underneath her to unfasten the hooks. Muttering something Verity couldn't catch, he ripped away the flimsy covering and buried his face in their softness, his lips tender at first and then more demanding as he felt the hardening of her taut, pink nipples.

Verity lay back, her eyes closed, whimpering softly as he explored her body, pulling away the rest of her clothes and then tearing at his own until they were both naked. There was a pause then as they looked at each other. Verity was aware of his eyes, almost reverent as they moved over her slender waist and gently curving hips, his hands touching her as if she were something fragile, moving lightly from the tips of her breasts to her flat stomach, to the fluff of golden hair and the silky skin of her thighs. But her own eyes were working too, taking in the muscular shoulders, the broad chest, covered with tangling black hair, tapering to a narrow waist and small, neat buttocks. She could see now the clamorous masculinity of his arousal, thrusting forward with an arrogance that belied the tenderness in his hands yet transmitted itself through their tension. And then simply looking wasn't enough any more for either of them, and as Verity reached up for him he came down to her, their skins meeting with an impact that she felt must surely be as blatant as the crash of cymbals, and for a moment they clung together, aware of every inch of contact, revelling in the sensation of skin against skin.

'Verity,' he muttered against her breasts. 'Oh, my God, Verity—I've dreamed about this for so long—I thought it would never happen.'

Verity lay under him, moving her hands across his shoulders and down to the small of his back, cupping her palms over the swell of his buttocks. Her heart had slowed its racing and was now pounding out a deep, steady rhythm as powerful as the primitive beat of jungle drums. She could feel him against her from her toes, which were tangling with his, through their entwining legs and up the length of their bodies which moved together with an ardent need to come ever closer. His lips were moving over her with a desperate urgency, covering her breasts, her neck, her face with kisses that seemed as if they would burn through to her very soul. The depth of his need, transmitting itself through skin and nerves, muscle and bones, called out an equal need in her that was frighteningly intense. For a moment Verity wondered just what would happen if—when—they both let go completely. Could anyone survive the storm that had to follow, the inevitable tempest of such lovemaking? But it was no longer something she could control; she could only let it sweep her along, go where he took her, submerge herself in him until their clamouring bodies were satisfied at last.

And in a small part of her brain, the part that never really stops working, she knew that this was a watershed in Struan's own development, that if she did not handle his heart with care at this moment he would never really recover. He was opening himself to her as he never had before, to any woman. To betray him would be unforgivable.

But she wasn't going to betray him, in any way. From tonight on, they would belong wholly to each other, whatever might happen. Tonight was the consummation of something that had begun five years ago.

'Verity . . .' Struan murmured again, and she turned her face to his and gave him her lips, opening them to his so that their tongues could meet and mingle, so that each warm, moist crevice could be explored. Tiny whimpers sounded in her throat as she clung even tighter, letting her body move against his so that the friction of naked skin sent surges of delight coursing through her veins. Every smallest muscle was coming into play now, flexing, contracting, so that at each point there was a constantly varying pressure, a sensuous reminder that there was no part of the body that could not evoke an erotic response. There was no time to wonder how she knew this, only a certainty that what she was doing was right, that her instincts could be trusted, her mind give way to her body. And to Struan's body, she thought with a shiver of pure excitement, and flung her head back with a moan as Struan's lips left hers and travelled down to her breasts, to the taut flatness of her stomach, and finally to the warm shadows of her thighs.

'Struan . . .' His head was coming back now to hers, and he caught her closely in his arms and rolled on to his back, taking her with him so that she lay astride him, looking down at his face, at the damp tendrils of black hair on his forehead. Verity stretched her body to his, sliding her hands up his arms so that they were held above his head, and they lay together like a cross, making tiny, sensuous movements that had both hearts thundering, driving themselves on with a mounting excitement that became almost intolerable. 'Struan ...' she whispered again, lowering her face to his and laying her lips against the mouth that had lost all its grimness now. 'Struan, I can't bear it—it's too much ...'

'Ssh ...' He was holding her away from him now, rolling her over again so that she lay once more on her back. But this time he didn't cover her, didn't press his body against hers. Instead, he began a leisurely caressing that calmed her, letting his hands move gently over her skin, avoiding the most sensitive parts until her breathing steadied and she was smiling at him. They looked into each other's eyes, darkest sapphire meeting glinting silver, and she reached up to stroke his face, tracing the lines of brow and forehead and proud, aquiline nose with a wonder that they were really together at last, that nothing now could come between them. And then she saw his eyes darken once more, the silver become a shimmering rim to a pupil widening with desire that this time would not be calmed. His fingers began a more urgent exploration, creating tiny points of a rapture so exquisite she could hardly tolerate it, a focus of tender agony that had her twisting and squirming in his arms. Once again, her breath was coming quickly, her mind reeling as she clung to his body, no longer able to caress him, no longer able to do anything but gasp out his name, over and over again. 'Struan, Struan, Struan ... oh, Struan ...'

'Now,' he whispered, and drove his knee between her twisting thighs. Once again, his body was on hers, this time thrusting deep into her, an arrogant intrusion that was at first a shock which forced from her a cry of disbelief. It took her a moment or two to recognise and

accept the new sensation; it was like nothing she had
ever experienced before, a fullness that suddenly seemed
right, as if there had always until now been a part of her
that was missing. With an involuntary movement she
gripped him to her, twisting her legs round his back;
and then, as he gave a small grunt of satisfaction, began
to move with him in a rhythm that needed no teaching,
a rhythm that her body seemed to know and have been
waiting for. It quickened, beating faster and faster
through her blood, a throbbing, pulsing force that
seemed to have taken them both over, turning them
from two separate people into one new, complete being.
This was what life was *for*, Verity thought in a flash of
clarity, this was what it was all about ... And then
there was an explosion that shook them both, an
explosion that seemed to go on and on, shuddering
through their bodies, obliterating all other thought and
feeling so that there was nothing but this, this terrifying,
wonderful, awesome manifestation which could only
happen where there was true, deep love.

They calmed at last, gradually returning to a gentler
mood and finally lying together in an exhaustion that
flooded their limbs and brought them to a heavy
languor. Struan kissed her tenderly, smoothed back her
damp, darkened hair with one hand, lifted her head on
to his shoulder. Verity lay still, delighting in the
continuing feel of his skin against hers even though the
shattering excitement had gone. Its place had been filled
by a warm contentment, which was all she wanted now.
And it would come back; she knew it would come back.

'I always knew it would be right with you,' Struan
murmured at last. 'But I never dreamed it could be
quite like that ... Verity, I love you so much.'

'And I love you,' she whispered, finding the words
easy to say now, and deeply thankful that she had never
said them to any other man. Fleetingly, she wondered

what would happen next. But it was too soon to think of that. This was their night, hers and Struan's. It could not be spoiled by thoughts of tomorrow, when a harsher world would intrude.

There was one thing she had to know, though, and she took a deep breath to ask the question.

'Struan—Gina, will she—will she miss you if she wakes?' It hurt even to remind him of the world that waited for them, but she had to do it. 'Will she expect you to be there?'

'My God, no!' His response was involuntarily shocked. 'We don't share that room, Verity, don't think that. We're divorced, remember—and even before that . . .' He turned his lips to hers and murmured against them, 'I'll stay with you till morning, my heart—if that's what you want.'

There was no need to ask that. Verity, curled against him and already half asleep, heard his words with a warm delight. Till morning . . . and a night could be a long, long time. It would be enough simply to sleep in Struan's arms . . . if that was what he wanted.

But it wasn't. And by the time Verity finally fell asleep, somewhere around dawn, her thoughts had been lost in a continuing ebb and flow of erotic pleasure that had taken them by storm again and again, driving itself into their dreams so that neither of them was ever quite sure what had been real and what imagined. Except that of course it must all have been real; as real as the love they felt for each other, the love they had recognised at that first meeting and had been forced to suppress for five long, arid years.

Struan left her with a kiss as the morning birdsong was at its height, a twittering cacophony of gaiety which heralded a summer of love, of nesting and family-raising. And that really is what it's all about, Verity thought again drowsily as she slipped back into sleep. Nothing else matters quite so much.

And nothing, surely, could come between her and Struan now. Whatever problems they had to face, their love could overcome them. Nothing could resist such a powerful, primitive force.

Afterwards, she wondered how she could have been so naïve.

CHAPTER TEN

GINA did not get up until lunchtime again next day, and when she did come downstairs Verity was shocked by her appearance. The pale face was thinner than ever, the eyes sunken hollows, the blonde hair wispy and straggling. The fact that she had obviously done what she could to regain her glamour, draping her gaunt body in a dress that had once been close-fitting but now hung on her, and making up her face with a care which resulted only in grotesqueness, simply made her look more pathetic. As Verity watched, she was filled with sudden pity.

'Oh, hello, Verity.' Gina was obviously determined not to acknowledge that anything was wrong. She lit a cigarette with fingers that shook, and blew out the first puff of smoke. 'How are you this morning? Sorry I was a bit off-colour.' She moved over to the window, her reddened lips outlining the dreadfully artificial smile on her face—a smile that Verity could see masked bewilderment and despair.

She felt helpless and inadequate. How did one cope with a woman who was going through the torment that Gina was obviously suffering? She couldn't be condemned for what had happened to her. Losing the man she loved, having to marry his brother, giving birth to their child only to be hit by post-natal depression ... how many women could have survived such a tragic history? And there was no easy solution—only a slow haul back to health and perhaps some compromise at the end of it. It was impossible to see what that might be.

There's no place for me in all this, Verity thought
with a sudden desolation. The way Struan and I feel
about each other—powerful though it is—can't have
anything to do with the problem of his marriage to
Gina. It can only make everything worse.

Gina was over by the window now, dragging
furiously at her cigarette. Her whole body was shaking
as if she were chilled to the bone, and she wrapped thin
arms round herself as if in an effort to stop the
trembling. She turned again with the abrupt, nervous
movement that Verity was coming to know.

'God, I need a drink,' she muttered. 'Can't you help
me, Verity? Can't you get me something?'

'Gina, I'm sorry, I can't—Struan told me it affects
your medication and——'

'Oh, I know, I know. Nobody will help me.' The
cracked voice rose in a cry of despair. 'They all *say* they
want to help, but what do they do? They just make me
feel worse! Tablets, pills, medicines—how can they help
when all I want is a *drink*?'

Verity went towards her. Gina was shaking uncontrollably now, the tears pouring down her face and
streaking the thickly-applied make-up. She looked at
Verity piteously, and Verity suddenly thought of Lucy
when she had been refused something she'd set her
heart on. Gina was just a child, she thought
compassionately, and without any more hesitation she
took Gina in her arms and held her.

At her first touch, Gina broke down completely, and
Verity led her across to the sofa and lowered her on to
it, sitting beside her in order to cradle the shuddering
body against her own. Perhaps it was the best thing, to
let Gina cry; perhaps when she had cried herself out she
would have forgotten her craving for drink and be able
to see more clearly what her real need was. Although
that might not be much help, Verity thought wryly,

since Gina's real need was for something she could never have.

But we all lose at some point in our lives, she reflected. And most of us cope without coming to this. It *can* be done.

It seemed a long time before Gina lifted her head, and before that Verity was conscious of Mrs Weedon coming in, giving them a quick glance and going out again. Presumably the housekeeper understood the situation, and would give Lucy her lunch and keep her out of the room. She continued to sit quietly holding the sobbing Gina, stroking her hair and waiting.

At last Gina drew a deep, shuddering breath and shifted away from Verity's arm.

'My God,' she said, searching for a handkerchief, 'what a mess I am.'

Verity found her own handkerchief and gave it to her. 'Would it help to talk about it? I do know the basic story—Struan told me.'

'Did he?' Gina nodded, apparently not minding this. Perhaps she was accustomed by now to having her history recounted to outsiders—doctors, specialists, nurses and so on. 'Well, then you probably know all there is to know. Including the fact that whatever travesty of a marriage there ever was between Struan and me has been completely destroyed without setting either of us free.' She wiped her swollen eyes, staring hopelessly round the room. 'Struan and I are tied together for the rest of our lives, Verity, and I think that's probably the worst part of it.'

'Because of Lucy?'

'Oh, Lucy's a part of it, I suppose. She's a Courtney, after all, and I couldn't take her away from here. Not that I'd want to . . . I'm not the world's best mother, as you may have noticed. But there's more than that. Struan took me when I needed someone most, and somehow I can't break that tie. I know our marriage doesn't exist any more—but there's something else that does, something that I can't explain but that's as strong as any bond of love.' She shrugged helplessly. 'I've tried to leave him so many times—gone back to London, taken up with my old friends, taken lovers even—but I always come back. I have to.'

Verity stared at her. You and me both, she thought bitterly, but knew that, although the bond between her and Struan was of love, Gina held the stronger position. Because for the past five years Verity had been developing a strength that had enabled her to stand alone, while Gina had been as steadily disintegrating.

Struan would never abandon this wreckage that had once been his wife. Nor would Verity ever ask him to.

'But your depression?' she said tentatively, not sure whether Gina was ready to admit she had a problem. 'Has nobody been able to help?'

Gina shrugged. Her despair had been momentarily relieved by the tears she had shed, and she was as near normal now as she could ever be. 'They try. I've been in hospitals, nursing homes, had all the usual treatment . . . It will only work, they tell me, if I want it to, if I co-operate. But what's the point?' Her voice rose again. 'What's the point of wanting to, when there isn't anything else? When there's nothing and no one—only an ex-husband who never wanted me in the first place, and a daughter who thinks of nothing but damned rabbits!'

'But there *is* something else,' Verity said. 'There's you. You've got your*self*, Gina—isn't that worth something? And when you come down to it, it's all any of us really have—ourselves. Aren't we all worth something? Aren't *you* worth something?' Dimly, she remembered Struan saying similar words to her, years ago when she had been shy and diffident, feeling herself overshadowed by a glamorous older sister. 'You're unique, Gina,' she urged. 'There isn't anyone else like you—and you're *valuable*. Yes——' She caught at the other girl's bitter protest. 'I mean it. You can be valuable to someone—even if you haven't found him yet. There's *life* out there, Gina, and you could be sharing it. You *ought* to be sharing it.'

'Life!' Gina said bitterly. 'It hasn't done much for me so far.'

'So give it another chance. Stop letting it blow you about and take control yourself. It makes a lot of difference—and that's something I *do* know.' Verity squeezed the unresponsive hands. 'Try again, Gina. Struan will help you, I know he will. Don't you realise, he never wanted you to be unhappy. Why do you think he married you?'

'Oh, that's easy,' Gina said, showing a spark of life at last. 'He married me for the child. He thought it might be a boy, an heir for the estate. If I hadn't been pregnant, he wouldn't have given me a thought.'

Verity stared at her. Could she really believe that? Hadn't she ever properly understood Struan's reasons for marrying her?

'But it wasn't like that at all!' she cried. 'Struan didn't marry you because he wanted your baby—because he thought it might be a son to inherit the estate. He married you because he thought the baby *ought* to inherit—because it was Justin's son, and if you and Justin had married the baby *would* have inherited. It was to make sure of justice for the child that Struan married you. And for you too—so that you still had the home and position that you'd have had as Justin's wife. Don't you understand that? Didn't he ever tell you?'

'I don't know what he told me,' Gina said wearily. 'I wasn't in much of a state to take things in. I was glad enough to accept his offer at the time—but I was already having doubts by the wedding-day. And judging by the honeymoon we had, so was he!'

Verity remembered Struan's haunted eyes, his desperation as he'd held and kissed her in the lane . . . Yes, he had known then it wasn't going to work. Perhaps Gina had too. But neither of them could have turned back.

'Won't you try again, Gina?' she urged gently. 'I'll help, if you want me to. And I know Struan will.'

Gina looked at her, then sighed, letting her shoulders sag. 'I suppose so. There's not much else I can do, is there? I know you're right—I'll kill myself if I go on like this. Perhaps that's what I'm trying to do.'

'Don't—please don't talk like that. Just tell Struan you want to try again. And go back to your doctor. He'll help too.'

Gina shrugged, but there was a light in her dull eyes that hadn't been there before, a new purpose in her movements as she got up and stood looking down at Verity. Had that been the root of it all along, Verity wondered—the thought that Struan had cared nothing for her or the child but that it should be a son to inherit the estate? Had it really never occurred to her that Struan was quite capable of fathering his own son— that he didn't have to rely on his brother to do it for him . . .?

Gina went to the door, a frail, haggard figure, and Verity wondered if she would ever again become the chocolate-box girl she had been a few years ago. 'Tell Mrs Weedon I'll have lunch in my room. Just something light—scrambled egg or something like that. And then I'll have a sleep. I feel—somewhat shattered.'

She left the room and Verity sank back against the cushions. She too felt shattered—swept by a sick exhaustion that left her feeling too weak to move. The past twenty-four hours, she reflected, had been rather a lot to cope with.

And now, just what had she done? Set Gina on the road to recovery? If she had, it was a long, hard road, and one that Gina would need a lot of help to travel. And Verity knew just whose help she would need most.

Which left Verity herself—just where?

The rest of the day passed quietly. It stopped raining, and Verity took Lucy out for a walk, climbing the hill behind the house so that they could look out over the surrounding countryside. Rolling fields fell away from the slopes, freckled with bushes and, here and there, a small valley made secret with thick woods. Away from the hill, where the ground was more fertile, the fields were larger and planted with corn which was now tall and green, shaded with rippling colour as a breeze drifted across it. Villages clustered in hollows, each one dominated by a church, the thatched roofs of the cottages looking like the bent heads of a congregation.

Somewhere down there, Struan was working. Either out in the fields, visiting one of his farms, or busy in his office. It was one of the things that Verity admired about him, his capacity for hard work. He didn't really need to work so hard; the estate was productive enough to keep Courtneys maintained and the family in comparative luxury without Struan's efforts—he could have employed a manager and spent his time enjoying a life of leisure, travelling abroad, even living there. No doubt that was what Justin would have done—and, in that case, Gina too. Had Struan ever considered that? Had he ever realised that in marrying Gina he had trapped her in a way of life she probably hated?

But perhaps he was driven to the solace of hard work because of his home situation. Perhaps, married

to the right woman, he would have achieved a more
balanced existence. Spent time with his wife and
family . . .

The thought of Struan with a family caught at
Verity's heart. It would be *her* family too, she thought
with a sudden plunge into desolation. The family that,
now, neither of them would ever have . . .

Calling Lucy, who was exploring a hollow tree for
owls' nests, she began to make her way back down the
hill. Courtneys lay below, small by many country-house
standards but still large to her, its Cotswold stones
mellow in the afternoon sunlight. The walls were
covered with roses and wistaria, the terrace dotted with
brightly-flowering tubs. The lawns stretched away,
green and smooth, and she could see Mrs Weedon
crossing to the white table and yellow sun umbrella,
carrying a tray. Tea, for Gina no doubt. It looked
idyllic, she thought. Nobody could possibly have
guessed at the agony those mellow walls had witnessed.

On a sudden impulse, she led Lucy away from the
path that led back to the grounds, and followed one to
the next village instead. There was a cottage which
served teas; here they would refresh themselves instead
of going home. Lucy was delighted with the idea—she
had been there before with her previous nanny, and
knew the owner well. And it was clear from the
reception that the dumpling-shaped owner knew Lucy
too.

'Well, if it isn't little Lucy, from over Courtneys!
You're a stranger, and no mistake. Haven't been to see
us for weeks, have you, my dear? I was beginning to
think you didn't like my cakes and buns no more.'

'Of course I do. That's why we've come. We want a
big plateful, please. This is Verry,' Lucy added with a
casual wave of one small hand at Verity.

'Verity Sandison. I'm looking after Lucy for a while,'

Verity smiled. 'And we'd like some tea, please—a pot for me, and what do you want to drink, Lucy?'

'Milk-shake,' Lucy said without hesitation. She continued to chatter as the small, round woman brought their tea, pointing out which were the best cakes and insisting that Verity should have small pieces of the ones she chose herself, so that she'd have tried them all. Verity watched her eat, wondering what effect Gina's homecoming was having on the child. She seemed normal and happy enough now, but Verity hadn't missed her silence when Gina was around. Lucy seemed to shrink into herself when she was with her mother, and that couldn't be good.

All the same, she couldn't keep the child out for ever, and eventually she interrupted the flow of talk, paid for their tea and took Lucy out to begin the walk back home.

They had not gone far when a Land Rover drew up beside them and she recognised Struan.

'Daddy! Daddy, did you come to look for us? We've been having tea at Mrs Bartley's.' Lucy scrambled up beside him, her face alight. 'I had a meringue and an Eccles cake and Verry had a piece of gingerbread and a chocolate sponge, didn't you, Verry? We're both full up now.'

'I imagine you must be.' Struan's smile was warm as he answered his daughter, but when he turned his eyes to Verity she saw with a shock that they were icy cold. She blinked and hesitated. What had gone wrong?

'Well, are you getting in or not?' His voice was cold too, clipped with impatience. 'You can walk home if you'd rather.'

For a moment, Verity thought she would much rather, but she shook off the idea and climbed up beside Lucy. Struan turned away as though he were completely indifferent to her presence, letting out the

clutch so that the Land Rover surged forward. His eyes
were fixed firmly on the road, and his mouth was grim.

What had happened? Verity wondered, a cold chill
around her heart. Why was he looking like that? Had
Gina told him about their conversation at lunchtime?
But even if she had—would *that* be any reason to look
so coldly furious?

It was only a mile to the gates of Courtneys, and
Struan drove the Land Rover right up to the house
instead of taking it round to the farm office as he would
normally have done. Lucy was out almost before he had
stopped, anxious now to feed her rabbits before they
began to wonder where she was, leaving Struan and
Verity alone.

'Struan——' she began hesitantly, still afraid of that
dark anger in his eyes, unable to equate it with the
desire she'd seen there only a few hours ago. 'Struan,
what is it? Has something happened?'

'You might say so.' His voice was hard, all tenderness
vanished. 'But I don't intend to talk about it here,
Verity. You'd better go indoors. I'll see you in the
drawing-room in twenty minutes.'

It was an order, brusque and unquestionable.
Silently, Verity climbed down from the Land Rover and
went indoors.

Her body felt cold, her mind numb. Just what had
happened to make Struan look at her like that? What
had changed him?

Struan was already in the drawing-room when Verity
came down, standing by the window. He turned as she
came in, his eyes raking her with a hard contempt that
was like a whip to her cringing flesh. As she hesitated
by the door, he flicked a hand in an impatient gesture
to come in.

'I suppose you're going to pretend you don't know

what this is about,' he began curtly, and Verity shook
her head.

'I'm not going to pretend anything. I *don't* know
what it's about. I've no idea what's the matter. Tell me,
Struan—it surely can't be anything we can't sort out.'

'A mere misunderstanding, you mean?' His lip curled.
'No, I don't think so, Verity. Quite the reverse, in fact. I
happen to have discovered the truth.'

'The truth? What truth?' She was dazed, unable to
understand what he was saying. Hadn't last night been
the truth?

'The truth about you.' He moved as if to cross the
room, then checked himself. 'You've been talking to
Gina, haven't you?'

'Yes.' Alarm suddenly kicked inside her. 'She—she's
all right, isn't she? She hasn't——'

'She's all right, as far as I know.' His tone was
suddenly weary. 'She's left Courtneys again. Gone back
to London, to her jetsetting friends, I suppose.' His eyes
were turned to her, suddenly filled with the torment
she'd seen before; then, as Verity made a movement
towards him, the shutters came down again, the blank
indifference returning. 'Well, maybe she's right at that.
Maybe the whole scene here is bad for her—maybe
she's better off out of it. Anyway, she's gone and there's
nothing I can do except wait for the next development,
whatever that might be. Not that it's really any of my
business, of course—she isn't my wife any more. I just
happen to feel responsible.'

Verity took a step forward. 'Please, Struan, don't
blame yourself. You did what you believed was right.
And it *was* right, I'm sure—for Lucy, if no one else. It's
Gina's own nature that's been fighting against you, that
and the things which have happened to her. None of it's
your fault.'

'Thank you for nothing.' His voice was harsh again.

'If there's one thing I *don't* need, it's your sympathy. Or was that the angle you were planning to use? The steel knife in the velvet glove. The sympathetic approach, while all the time you're driving your dagger deeper into my back.'

Verity stared at him. 'I don't know what you're talking about.'

'Don't you? Don't you?' Now he did cross the room, taking three savage strides to reach the low table where there was a pile of Gina's glossy magazines. 'Are you really denying that you wrote these articles?' He ripped through the gaudy pages, reading out each title in a voice that was shot with bitterness. *'The Truth Behind The Pop Scenes: Michael Jennings As Nobody Else Has Seen Him. Post-Natal Depression—A Case History.* And what about this one—*Today's Woman As An Alcoholic*? Is that what you told Gina—that she's an alcoholic? After all I'd told you——'

Verity closed her eyes. Why, *why* hadn't she told him the truth about herself? Why had the moment never seemed right to tell him about her career as a journalist?

'Please, Struan,' she said desperately, 'don't jump to conclusions. Those articles—they're responsible, truthful articles about things that matter today. Oh, some matter more than others, I agree. What happens behind the scenes in the pop world may not be quite so vital as alcoholism or drugs. But they can have quite a lot to do with each other. And that article on alcoholism is the result of a lot of careful research. I try to *help* people by writing what I do—not damage them.'

'You really do?' His voice was incredulous. 'The revelations about the latest heart-throb and the life he tries to keep private—you really think that helps anyone? Oh, let's stop pretending, Verity—let's get at the truth now about why you actually came here. Can you honestly deny that you were in search of a story?'

'A story?' Her mind was blank.

'Yes, a story. Don't pretend to misunderstand me. You knew about me, you knew about my marriage to Gina and about Justin. Or if you didn't know the facts, you had a pretty good idea what had happened. Who better than you to find out? You were in an ideal position to look back through old newspapers and magazines, to delve in old files, find out all about the sort of man Justin was and the girls he was going around with. You knew—God forgive me—that I wasn't happy about the marriage. You knew how I'd felt about you. And you decided to come back. Use the attraction you'd had for me, find out what my life was now, see if there was a story in it.' He threw the magazines down and paced to the other end of the room. 'And what a story you found! Desperate husband, depressed wife, still tied together in spite of a divorce—my God, they'll pay you well for this! You even managed to get me into your bed just to prove what kind of man I am. Will you write it all up, I wonder? Will you include your own reactions—the way you moaned and twisted in my arms, the way you begged for more, the way you——'

'*No!* Stop it!' Verity covered her ears, but she could still see Struan's face, distorted with bitterness, his eyes blazing with tormented rage as he came towards her. Terrified, she stared at him. She could see that he was on the brink of losing all control, that by staying here within his sight she was acting as an intolerable goad to his precarious temper.

There was nothing she could say to him, no way she could explain now. If only she had told him earlier, perhaps he could have accepted her assurances. But now it was too late. Struan had been through too much and he was beyond reason.

With a choking cry, Verity turned and ran from the room.

CHAPTER ELEVEN

IT was oddly quiet in Sophie's and Ed's New York apartment, when you thought how close it was to the centre of the throbbing city. But there was a limit to how far sound could travel upwards, and with wide double-glazed windows there wasn't really much chance for the noise to penetrate.

Verity sat by one of the huge windows, staring down at the streets far below. Cars moved about like children's toys, people were foreshortened and tiny, like ants. Nothing could have been more different from the tranquillity of Courtneys, she thought. But it was equally deceptive. For the tranquillity of Courtneys was a lie, a façade which hid a seething nest of unhappiness and turmoil, while here in this apartment, surrounded by the modern jungle that was New York, there was nothing but joy and laughter.

Sophie had made a good marriage, and it had seemed so unlikely. Tall and laconic, Ed Carrington had swept her off her feet, uprooting her to live in America, in the middle of what was probably the busiest, noisiest city in the world. And Sophie obviously loved it, loved every minute of her hectic existence, and, more than anything else, loved Ed.

So much so that Verity had hesitated to impose on them. But her doubts had soon been brushed aside by an exuberant Sophie, who by now was more American than the Americans.

'Why, of course you can come on over and stay, honey,' she'd exclaimed when Verity rang her from London. 'As long as you like, yes, we'll love to have

174

you. Ed's always saying you ought to come over and try
your luck with the American magazines. Why don't
you give it a try while you're here? And if you find the
city a little too much for you at first, you can always go
and stay in our cottage in New Jersey.'

Reassured, Verity had packed her luggage and caught
the next flight to New York. She was aware that she was
running away—but she didn't care. The situation at
Courtneys was hopeless. Struan's love had turned to
hate, a black, angry hate that terrified her. There was
nothing she could do to change it, no way to persuade
him that she had never intended to use his private
agony as the basis for an article. If she had only told
him earlier that she was a journalist, that she had come
from a deep need to see him again, he might have
believed her. And if there had been more time, she
would have told him. But Gina's arrival had upset the
tenuous development of their relationship, had rushed
them to a climax that had come too soon. When Struan
made his discovery, it had seemed like a betrayal. She
could only hope that time would be on her side.

But, of course, it wouldn't. Time would make no
difference to the fact of his marriage and the effects of
its break-up. He would never totally abandon Gina
while she depended on him. Nor would Verity have
accepted him if he had.

New York, and Sophie, were just what she needed.
Between them, she was given no time to think or to
brood—she was swept up in a whirlwind of activity, of
sightseeing, of parties and theatres. If Sophie noticed
that there was anything the matter with her sister, she
gave no sign, merely listened when Verity felt like
talking and asked no questions. During the week they
shopped, met Sophie's friends and sat around the
apartment, talking, listening to music and watching TV.
At weekends, when Ed was free, they went to the

cottage, where Verity walked for miles along the beaches, letting the wind blow her hair free and praying for it to blow away her troubles as well. She began to feel better, the first agony of her flight from Courtneys starting to fade. At least, that was what she told herself, but she was aware that she was really only pushing it away. It was still there in the recesses of her mind, waiting to leap out at her when she wasn't expecting it. It caught her at odd moments, so that her eyes filled with tears at the sound of a certain strain of music, or a phrase from a song. It invaded her dreams, where she had no protection.

In busy streets, she would see someone who looked like Struan, crossing the road—and when she looked again, there was no resemblance at all. In a restaurant, she caught the tilt of a head three tables away and her heart stopped. In a theatre, the man in front of her ran his hand through his thick, black hair, and she had to stop herself from reaching out.

'I think I'll take you up on your suggestion,' she had said to Ed one morning at breakfast. 'Try a few feature articles here. Some of mine have already sold to one or two of your magazines—perhaps I ought to contact the editors, see if there's anything I could do.'

'Sure, but why don't you let me help you?' Ed asked the names of the magazines, and then grinned. 'Why, I know those guys. Let me take you along to lunch one day and introduce you. What do you say to tomorrow?'

Verity blinked. She hadn't expected such quick action. 'That—that would be fine,' she stuttered. 'So long as you don't mind——'

'Honey, haven't I been telling you to do just this for the past two years? New York's *ready* for you, Verity, don't you know that? Haven't you been a big success everywhere you've been?'

'Certainly she has, and she'll be a bigger one yet.'

Sophie brought muffins through and placed them on the table. She gave her sister a warm smile. 'Okay, hon, so you'll have to climb the ladder again. But this one starts where yours left off. You just step across from the top of one to the bottom of the other, right? And this one reaches the *sky*.'

'So long as I don't slide down an equally long snake,' Verity said with a smile, and the other two laughed.

'Well, you may find the odd rattler in American magazines, but I guess you can cope with them,' Ed told her, reaching for butter. 'Anyway, that's settled, okay? I'll fix lunch tomorrow, and then—why, then you'll *really* hit New York.'

And so she had. The editors remembered the articles they'd bought from Verity's agent, and were eager to give her commissions. There was room, they said, for an English point of view in their magazines, and the topics Verity covered were of interest to everyone, no matter what race or colour. And her profiles of celebrities would freshen up their pages. Before the lunch was over she had from one of the editors a promise of an interview with one of Broadway's top actors, together with an appointment with the other for the next day to discuss a series. 'I'm sorry I can't make it today,' he'd apologised, 'but it would have to be rushed, and I don't want to do that. I'll keep tomorrow afternoon free for you, though, and tell my girl I don't want any interruptions.'

Since then, Verity had had as much work as she could handle. Now, on a rare free afternoon, she was staring down at the street and wondering if it wasn't time she found herself an apartment of her own.

It wasn't an easy decision to make. Mainly because it wasn't the real decision, which was whether she meant to make her home in America. Or even whether she could. Verity wasn't too sure about the formalities, but she was pretty sure that her present visa didn't cover permanent residence. Presumably that could be changed, but . . .

But did she want to change it? Did she want to stay here, working on American magazines, turning her back on England and the life she'd made for herself there, the friends she had? The man she loved . . .?

Yes, that was the real point, wasn't it? Oh, how stupid can you be, Verity asked herself savagely. There isn't a chance now for you and Struan. Better to forget he ever existed. You almost managed it before. Can't you do it again?

And wouldn't staying here with an ocean between them make it easier?

But she knew that nothing was going to make it any easier. Time might help a bit, might fade some of the memories. But an awful lot of time was going to be needed. Because now there were so many memories. Memories of herself and Struan on the riverbank, with Lucy nearby catching fish in a yogurt pot. Memories of tea in the garden, coffee in the drawing-room, golden with sunset. Walks on the terrace, music in the gathering dusk. A day of careless freedom; a night of love so exquisite that she could hardly believe it had been real.

But it had happened, and for a while Verity had wondered if she might have proof of it. When she found there was to be no result from that tumultuous lovemaking, she hadn't known whether to be relieved or disappointed. But it was probably just as well. She could have coped with a baby, would have loved it because it was made from the love between her and Struan, would have given her life to it. But Struan?

How would he have reacted to the news, supposing he'd ever found out? A daughter that was really his? Or even a son . . .?

No, it was a complication that was better not to have

happened. And meanwhile, she still had to make up her mind what to do. She'd been here for nearly six months, and it was only fair to Ed and Sophie to make some decision.

Verity got up and went into the shining kitchen to make herself a coffee. As she did so, her eye caught the picture on the calender. It was the first of the month, and Sophie had turned it over that morning. The picture was of a large, lop-eared rabbit.

The tears flooded into her eyes and spilled over, falling down her cheeks, dripping on to her dress. She stared at the rabbit, her mind suddenly torn thousands of miles away to a kitchen garden where two adult rabbits and numerous young ones nibbled at grass in a wire cage. How many Macgregors were there now? she wondered with sudden bitter agony. And did Miss Morris—if she had ever come to take up her duties— enjoy looking after them, hearing about their exploits?

It was a moment or two before she registered the ring of the bell, and she rubbed her face with a towel before going to the door. There was an intercom to ask who was at the street door, and she used it, thinking that it was of little use when Sophie had so many friends and this could easily be one she'd never met. Nevertheless, she switched it on and asked who was there.

'I'd like to see Sophie Carrington,' a deep voice said, all characteristics wiped from it by the metallic sound of the intercom. 'Or Ed, if he's in.'

'I'm sorry, neither of them is here,' Verity said. 'I'm Sophie's sister, over from England. Can I help you?'

A pause, then the measured tones answered, 'I guess that's possible. Could I come up and talk with you for a while?'

Verity pressed the button and went back to the kitchen. No doubt the visitor would like coffee, Americans always did. By the time she heard him arrive, she had made it and was carrying it through to the living-room.

She set it down and went to the door, opening it with a smile she didn't really mean—and felt the shock hit her like a blow to the heart.

'Struan!'

He was almost filling the doorway, as tall and muscular as she'd remembered. His face was taut and unsmiling, his eyes glimmering like pewter. He was inside before she could move.

'That's me. Did you not recognise my voice?'

'Of course not,' she said weakly, falling back as he came towards her. 'You can't recognise anybody's voice with those things. Especially when they choose to disguise them. That was a very phoney American accent you put on.'

'Well, it fooled you for long enough.' He wasn't as relaxed as he wanted to appear, she thought, watching him across the room. In fact, he was about as nonchalant as a tiger stalking its prey. She shivered at the thought. Just why had he come here?

Struan had reached the window, his favourite position. She remembered him standing by the drawing-room window at Courtneys and closed her eyes against the pain.

'You're looking well,' he observed, contemplating her. His voice was deliberately casual, with the undercurrent of tension that went with the tightness of his body. 'I gather you're the toast of New York.'

'I can't imagine who told you that.' Why was he *here*, for God's sake?

'Can't you?' He shrugged, dismissing the question. 'You're doing well on the magazines, I understand. Articles, profiles, features—editors clamouring for your services. It must be very gratifying.'

'Look,' Verity said, trying to keep her voice under control, 'if you've just come here to taunt me, I——'

'Taunt you? I haven't the least intention of taunting you. You surely don't imagine I'd travel several thousand miles just to taunt you.' His face was drawn, she noticed, thinner than when she'd left as if life hadn't got any easier, and she felt a rush of hopeless love. Oh, if only she could go to him, put her arms around his neck, draw his head down to her breast. If only he would look at her, just once, as if he still had some feeling for her . . .

'So why did you come?' she asked in a whisper.

Struan regarded her bleakly, and she saw that the iron had gone from his eyes. He looked uncertain, lost. She took a step forward.

'I don't really know,' he said then, turning away. 'I don't really know why I came. Perhaps for the same reason that you came to Courtneys in the first place. To see what happened. To—to tie up some unfinished business.'

Verity stayed still. Instinctively, she knew that she must not touch him now. In the months since she had left, there had been some crisis—a crisis that was now resolved. Or Struan wouldn't have come to her. But that didn't mean the whole problem was solved. There was still obstacles in their path, they still had to tread with care.

'What's happened, Struan?' she asked quietly, and then, as he didn't respond, 'Sit down. Let's have some coffee. Let's just—be quiet for a while.'

He sat down then in the big armchair by the window, and Verity took a low stool opposite him. She poured coffee from the jug and returned it to the heater; she had an idea this might be a long job. Luckily neither Ed nor Sophie would be home for some hours, and they weren't likely to be interrupted.

Struan drank his coffee, staring absently from the window. Then he put the cup down and began to speak.

'First of all, Verity, I owe you an apology. I read your articles after you'd gone—after I'd calmed down—and I saw that they weren't the sensational muck-rakings that I'd expected. They were sober, responsible articles that sought to explain things to people who might be bewildered and worried, or who simply wanted to know. And your profiles—well, although you never pulled any punches, you were never snide or malicious. I realised, when I could think clearly again, that you weren't the type to come sneaking around for a story you could sell to the gossip-writers. I should have known it all along, of course—I just lost my reason for a while. I can only say I'm sorry.'

'It's all right,' Verity said after a moment. 'I realised that myself. But there didn't seem to be anything I could do about it. It was my fault anyway, for not having told you the truth.'

There was a short silence. Verity was finding this talk sharply painful. Emotions that she'd thought were safely battened down were having to be brought out again, examined in the cold light of day. That wouldn't matter if she could be sure that she wasn't going to end up even more bruised than before. But could she? It depended on why Struan had come here. Surely not only to apologise?

'Was there anything else?' she asked politely, and to her surprise he laughed—a natural, almost happy sound that brought an answering smile to her own face.

'You sound like a helpful shop assistant,' he said, and then sobered again. 'Yes, there is something else, Verity. I have a question to ask you. An important question. But first, I have to tell you what's been happening at Courtneys.'

'Yes—how's Lucy?' Verity leaned forward anxiously. 'She's all right, isn't she? I've wondered so often. I wanted to write to her but I thought—I thought you'd rather I didn't. I hope she wasn't too upset when I left——'

'She was. Extremely upset. I could only calm her by telling her you'd be back one day.' His eyes held hers. 'She doesn't know I've come to see you now, but if she did I know she'd send her love. And that of the Macgregors.'

'Oh, the Macgregors!' Verity remembered the lop-eared rabbit on the calendar. 'How many of them are there now?'

'Only a dozen or so. The others have—er—left home. Most of the village children have at least one rabbit now. Lucy's doing a roaring trade at school—she started in September.'

'And Miss Morris?' Verity blinked away the thought of Lucy starting school. 'Did she ever come?'

'Miss Morris came and is still with us. She's very good with Lucy, but unfortunately she can't stay long. She has an elderly mother and she wants to leave at Christmas to go and live with her.'

'Oh.' Verity digested this. Was this why Struan wanted to see her? But he surely didn't expect her to go back as Lucy's nanny? Not after all that had happened—and now that he knew the truth about her career?

'And now,' Struan said, moving his chair a little closer, 'can we stop this fencing? Can we get down to the real business?'

Verity looked at him mutely, her eyes dark blue pools in her pale face.

'What—what is the real business?' she asked faintly.

'The question of whether you're going to marry me,' he said.

How could she ever have thought the apartment quiet? There was a roaring in her ears that had to be the sound of traffic in the street below, a surging, throbbing, almost solid mass of noise which filled her mind. Verity covered her ears with her hands, but the sound only grew louder, and slowly, as the room stopped swinging, she realised that it was inside her own head.

It died away at last, and she dared to look at Struan. 'I—I think I misheard what you said,' she told him breathlessly. 'Would you mind repeating it?'

'I said, when are you going to marry me?' he repeated, not quite accurately.

'But I can't—you can't——' Bewilderment was turning her tongue to rubber. She shook her head, trying to clear it of the still throbbing noise that she knew now must be her own pounding heart. 'I don't understand.'

'No.' He sounded exasperated. 'I can't expect you to. I've said it all the wrong way round, and I'd got it all so clear in my mind, too. It's seeing you again, Verity—it drives all sense and reason from my brain. I just want to hold you in my arms and kiss you and let things happen naturally and whatever I say comes out wrong.'

Verity raised her head and looked at him, eyes bright. Why Struan had come here today and asked her to marry him, she didn't know—but at the moment she wasn't prepared to wonder. 'So why not try it that way?' she asked in a whisper. 'Hold me—kiss me—let things happen naturally.'

The table was knocked over as he came at her, the empty coffee-cups rolling harmlessly on the carpeted floor. Verity felt the breath crushed out of her as two powerful arms caught her against the lean, hard body. Before she could move she was lifted from her stool, held tightly, and then laid gently on the long, wide couch. She opened her eyes to see Struan leaning over her, his expression almost unbearably tender.

'You're right, Verity,' he said huskily. 'This is the

only way we can talk to each other. God, I was in despair just now—it was getting more like a business meeting with every word we uttered. I couldn't see any way out of it—but this is the way, the only way for us.'

He bent his head and kissed her, gently, undemandingly, but she could feel the passion tightening his lips. He sat up again, his fingers tracing a wondering line down her cheek.

'Now, perhaps I can get my thoughts straight enough to explain,' he said. 'First of all, Gina has married again.'

'Gina? *Married?*' Verity gave him a startled glance. It had been the last thing she expected to hear. Gina had seemed so dependent on Struan. And yet—maybe it wasn't Struan she was dependent on at all. Maybe any man would have done—any man strong enough to give her the care and love she needed.

'A month ago,' Struan confirmed. 'To someone she met after we were divorced. I don't like the man myself, but he seems to care for Gina and I think he'll look after her. And he'll give her the kind of life she seems to enjoy.'

'And—Lucy?'

'Lucy stays with me,' he said firmly. 'She's a Courtney through and through, and Gina doesn't want her—never did. And I accepted her as my daughter a long time ago. I don't see any reason to change that.' His eyes came back to Verity's face. 'Is that all right with you, Verity? Will you be happy for us to keep Lucy?'

'I haven't said I'll marry you yet,' she teased him, and saw his silvery eyes darken with an emotion that she recognised, and that caused her heart to jerk.

'But you will, won't you?' He lowered his mouth to hers, teasing her lips with tiny, elusive kisses, shaping her body with his hand until she was weak and trembling in his arms. 'You will. And then we can begin to make Courtneys what it ought to be. A home—a real, happy, family home.'

'A family home,' she repeated dreamily, sending all thoughts of her own New York apartment out of the window. She pictured Courtneys in all the seasons—spring and summer, the gardens filled with flowers. The woods painted with the brilliant, tawny shades of autumn; the stark, bare beauty of winter, with snow outlining the bony shapes of the trees. She saw Lucy, bending over a cot, taking the same delight in babies as she took in her family of Macgregors; and she saw a new generation of Courtneys growing up in the family home. Her eyes misted as she gazed into Struan's intent face, and then a spark of humour glinted somewhere in their depths. 'Do you want lots of children, Struan?' she whispered. 'I hope you do. Because I have a feeling we're going to breed like——' She paused and glinted another look up at him, catching the answering laughter in his own.

'Rabbits!' they finished together.

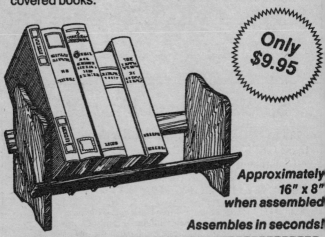

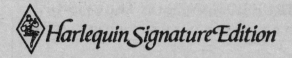

Harlequin Signature Edition

Carole Mortimer

Merlyn's Magic

She came to him from out of the storm and was drawn into his yearning arms—the tempestuous night held a magic all its own.

You've enjoyed Carole Mortimer's Harlequin Presents stories, and her previous bestseller, *Gypsy*.

Now, don't miss her latest, most exciting bestseller, *Merlyn's Magic*!

IN JULY

MERMG

All men wanted her,
but only one man would have her.

Her cruel father had intended
Angie to marry a sinister cattle baron twice her age.
No one expected that she would fall in love with his
handsome, pleasure-loving cowboy son.

Theirs was a love no desert storm would quench.

In August
Harlequin celebrates

The 1000th
Presents

Passionate Relationship

by
Penny Jordan

**Harlequin Presents,
still and always the No. 1 romance
series in the world!**

Available wherever paperback books are sold.